THE OTHER SIDE OF THE FARM

THE OTHER SIDE OF THE FARM

A novel

Yitzchak Goldman

TARGUM/FELDHEIM

First published 2003

Copyright © 2003 by Yitzchak Goldman
ISBN 1-56871-247-2

All rights reserved

No part of this publication may be translated, reproduced, stored in a retrieval system, or transmitted in any form or by any means, electronic, mechanical, photocopying, recording, or otherwise, without prior permission in writing from both the copyright holder and the publisher.

Published by:
TARGUM PRESS, INC.
22700 W. Eleven Mile Rd.
Southfield, MI 48034
E-mail: targum@netvision.net.il
Fax: 888-298-9992
www.targum.com

Distributed by:
FELDHEIM PUBLISHERS
202 Airport Executive Park
Nanuet, NY 10954
www.feldheim.com

Printed in Israel

לעלוי נשמת
חיה הדסה בת שמעון הכהן ע"ה

לעלוי נשמת
שאול בן דניאל הלוי ע"ה

In memory of

Leah Gershevna Yershkovich

and

Yakov Vatman

Acknowledgments

I am wholly indebted to HaKadosh Baruch Hu for His guidance in all aspects of this work. I would also like to express my gratitude to my wife and my family for their invaluable support and to Targum Press and the Seattle Kollel for the wonderful opportunity to give this message a platform.

Based on the allegory related by Rabbi Elchanan Wasserman, *zt"l*, before his martyrdom in 5701 (1941), in response to the thorny question: Why?

1

A Beautiful Field

Golias's eyes were giant marbles spinning and bumping clumsily against each other. His mouth was a gaping cave like the one down at Clayton Beach last summer. His armor was heavy but loose-fitting — it was difficult to keep tin foil securely in place.

"Ha! Ha! You're just a boy," Golias boomed from his precipice on box number 4.

It was a long way across to box number 7, a narrower, rougher platform where David stood, armored with only his sling and a few choice pebbles from the backyard.

"I'm not afraid of you," David said calmly, rolling the pebbles between his fingers. "Hashem is going to fight for me. I don't need to be strong like you, because Hashem is going to help me, just like Rabbi Menkin said."

Meanwhile, the Philistines, a conglomerate of Lincoln Logs,

were cheering loudly behind Golias on box number 4. One or two of them actually fell off momentarily because of the commotion, but were immediately replaced with little or no damage sustained.

Bnei Yisrael on the other side, resplendent in their post–World War II khaki combat gear, were nervous, chattering to each other, deliberating over the monstrous size of their enemy, Golias, and the glaring vulnerability of their representative, David.

Suddenly Golias moved forward, pummeling the box that strained to bear him, shaking every inch of the Philistine camp. Even the Philistines themselves stepped back in fear, finding it difficult to behold the power of the weapon they had themselves unleashed. Those who fell off the back of the box this time would not be rescued. There was too much going on.

David quickly but quietly went into action. A pebble was placed inside the sling, flew through the air, and struck Golias directly between the eyes.

"Ow!" Golias yelled, and he fell to the floor with a giant thud.

All at once *Bnei Yisrael* jumped from their positions, about to pursue their enemy across a multitude of mountainous boxes and a plethora of plains and valleys that lay between them, when a foreign sound that did not belong to any part of this scene disrupted the proceedings.

It was a female voice, almost certainly...motherly.

"Danny, what are you doing?" his mother said in an exasperated tone. "The movers are going to be here any minute. I asked you to pack away your toys in that box over there, not to play with them! Please, Mommy has a lot to do. I need your help, Danny. There's..."

She couldn't finish her sentence because a discussion had ensued in the dining room as to how the dining-room table would fit through the door, since it seemed that at every angle the table was far wider than the doorframe. Bubby Chana was voicing her fears over this (and every other) dilemma, convinced that there was no real solution short of the miraculous. Zeidy Mendel reminded her that the table had somehow gotten into the house in the first place, but this line of reasoning, as valiant an attempt as it was, could not placate Bubby Chana. The raised voices prompted Danny's mother to abruptly redirect her attention toward the dining room.

"Ahem. This is not something we should be worrying about right now," she said, flustered. Only moments ago she had been the pleading parent. Now she was the pleading child. "The movers will take care of that. That's what they are hired to do. Right now we need to concentrate on packing the rest of the stuff. Menachem needs help in the garage. He's not done with the garden tools yet."

Distress in a grown child's voice works wonders on Jewish parents, and at once Bubby and Zeidy complied. Danny could hear his *zeidy* making his way to the garage and his *bubby* scrambling for more boxes to pack the last few kitchen supplies that had been left out for the day of the move.

Danny stared down at Golias, now totally deflated, his marble eyes scattered and his tinfoil armor crumpled from the fall. The Philistine Lincoln Logs lay in a heap behind box number 4, which Danny was sure contained all his Rebbe cards, school drawings, and homemade menorahs. They had been plucked from their regular places, and now he did not recognize his room.

Every night, ever since he could remember, as he drifted to sleep, the small worn fold on the top left corner of his *Krias Shema* poster was there in the silence. But now it was in box number 7. On its shelf, the little carrot-colored teddy bear with the narrow black currant eyes would turn into an owl in the dark and stare straight at him, waiting for him to fall asleep. That was also in a box, but Danny wasn't sure which one. The chocolate-colored curtains that would lift slightly in the breeze coming through the opening in the long narrow window were also folded away somewhere.

He wasn't sure if he understood this moving business, why everything had to change like this. His rebbe also seemed sad about it, but he told Danny that wherever he went Hashem would go, too, to which Danny had responded, "Even to Grandridge? My father says it's a very small town."

And Rabbi Menkin had responded, "Yes, Danny, even to Grandridge."

He really did not want to put his toys away, but he did it anyway. Everything fitted in the box except for Golias's chariot, a 1971 Ford Mustang. The trunk jutted out, and Danny couldn't close the box no matter how hard he tried. He would enlist his father's help. Surely this noble cause would appeal to him.

Danny raced to the garage, calling for his father. There was no one in the garage. He spun around several times to make sure. He called out again, and there was no response. Maybe they had already moved, leaving him behind. A familiar panic spread through him, the kind that seized him in supermarkets when he wound up in a different aisle from that of his mother. The store would suddenly transform into an inescapable maze, a cruel trap that closed off all exits and dissolved all alleys of escape, so that he would be alone in a blend of reality and nightmare. And then he would spot his mother. The nightmare would crumble, and the store would just as quickly become a mere supermarket again.

He ran back through the basement and up the stairs, now in search of his mother. He shouted for her. If she did not respond, he would really be in trouble. But she did answer him, from the baby's room. She was nursing Yosef.

"What's wrong, Danny?" she asked quietly as she rocked back and forth with her precious bundle on the last piece of furniture in the room.

"Mommy, I can't find Tatty. He's gone!"

"No, no. The moving truck came. He's outside in the front with the movers."

"Oh."

"You want to see the truck?"

Danny's eyes widened. Before he could respond, his legs carried him down the hall, clearing the two steps joining the hall with the small foyer near the front door. Then the truck enveloped his sight, an enormous block that seemed to have swallowed up the entire front yard. He had often imagined something appearing and swallowing up the front yard – that and other countless exciting calamities like Noach's flood, which would lap against the walls of the house and force his father to take him to school by boat, or a snowstorm that would never stop, forcing his father to carve a giant-walled path down the walk.

"Tatty!" Danny called, the excitement bursting from him.

His father held out his hands absent-mindedly to receive him, his eyes focused on the dining-room table, which had been carried out of the house through the wide living-room window and was now being hoisted onto the truck. They both stared, Danny captivated by the riveting sight, his father burdened by his painful decision — the knowledge that he was taking his family away from all they knew, the city that bustled with religious life, a whole compendium of kosher offerings and tastes, minyanim on every block, and the proverbial "*Shkoi'ach!*" and "*Shalom aleichem*" that peppered most conversations.

Not that these did not exist in Grandridge, a small town just over an hour away situated on a high plateau near the mountains. It was a town that had originally stood alone with its own unique country charm but was now trying to escape the clutches of the ever-expanding metropolis creeping up on it like morning glory.

A Jewish community did exist there, with all the basic Jewish necessities, but it was a far cry from where they were now. What it did offer, though, was much more affordable living, which was key at this point, when Menachem was wallowing in red zeroes. And it was not all that far away from the city, a fact that the residents of Grandridge preferred to ignore, but a draw for the city-dwellers who wanted to keep a foot in their urban origins.

*   *   *

It was late in the afternoon when the truck and the two cars that were following it pulled up outside the slightly larger house in

Grandridge. It stood on the furthest edge of the town, where the line between town and countryside was blurred. Space between houses was much larger, and open fields were clearly visible all around. Prices were even lower here, and the hope was that the area would develop, promising a substantial return on their investment.

Danny had fallen asleep in the car, but when the engine sputtered out, the sudden silence jolted him awake. The adults were in the midst of a discussion, and he could see his father searching for his siddur as he spoke.

The new house beckoned. Danny stepped out of the car and squinted up at the house through the glare of the setting sun. There were tall, thin wooden beams on either side of the door. An assessment was made there and then as to the suitability of their use as firemen's poles like those that he had at his school — his old school. His mother, for some reason, was opposed to the idea.

Danny stepped onto the porch. The wood creaked under his sneakers, prompting him to bounce back and forth on his heels so that the creaking sound would become louder. A flurry of images filled his head, of old, crusty treasure chests hidden under the wood in a labyrinth of tunnels and caves and the challenge of locating the trapdoor that would unearth this secret network. Perhaps there were people there already, going about their lives with the wood as their sky. He immediately dropped to his knees, placing his ear to the floor, searching for any signs of clandestine activity.

"What are you doing, Danny?" a tired-looking Bubby Chana asked, more by rote than out of concern over the antics of her imaginative grandson.

She turned the key of the door and opened it so that the movers could start bringing in the furniture. Danny leaped up and ran inside. His mission of discovering the world under the wood gave way instantly to a new one — exploring every corner of the new house.

The rooms were large and the ceilings high. Danny sailed along the floor and leaped onto the staircase, which was old and a little rickety. But it was adorned in a thick velvet carpet that absorbed his footsteps. He scraped his fingernails along the carpet on one of the steps and was delighted that it displayed substantial potential for creative design.

Upstairs was dark and musty. It was so intensely quiet up there, he almost felt afraid. Well, not afraid, just a little nervous. He decided to forge ahead and face the darkness. The sun had disappeared over the horizon, and it was definitely that time of night that ushered in the black shadowy pangs of uncertainty, the kind that only the appearance of his mother or father at his bedside could alleviate. These new rooms seemed to seethe with this crawly eeriness.

Danny's heart beat slightly faster than usual. He began to wonder if there were still people left in the house in some corner of these dark rooms, forgotten in some dreadful mix-up. They would wait forever, like the time his father came so late to pick him up from baseball, when the field seemed to drain of all people and sounds of life and he was left alone.

He inched forward, concerned he might bump into someone. Was that breathing he could hear? Was that the thumping of his own heart — or someone else's?

Something struck his forehead. The gut-wrenching scream that pierced the entire house brought Danny's parents and grandparents, and even the movers, who were in the midst of resettling that obnoxious dining-room table. Only Yosef remained downstairs, playing cheerfully in his infant seat.

Danny's father switched on the lights, and his mother picked him up. After showing Danny that "the people" weren't there, he calmed down. Zeidy Mendel pointed to the cord of the window blinds. It was swaying gently in the breeze coming through the crack in the window, and the bottom of the cord reached down to about the same height as Danny's head. Danny was glad the mystery was solved, but it did not stop him from insisting on sleeping in his mother's bed that night.

He waited silently while the movers set up the beds in his parents' new bedroom. All he wanted now was to go back home. The adventures of the day had certainly been entrancing, but in the end the magic turned sour. He wanted to return to his bed in his old room with the *Krias Shema* poster and the carrot-colored teddy bear and file away the day with all his other temporary excursions into fantasy.

🌿 🌿 🌿

Yosef's cries cut into the early-morning quiet, but were soon accompanied by other sounds — animal noises. Danny's eyes darted open. The animals at the city zoo were behind bars. Were these animals behind bars? His mother rose to nurse the baby. His father was still sleeping soundly, apparently undisturbed by the fact that everything was new, that everything was different.

Danny stared up at the ceiling. A long crack wound its way like a stream down the center, past the dusty light fixture.

"Tatty, can we go home?" he whispered, staring into his father's face.

His father's eyebrows lifted momentarily, then dropped, his breathing pattern unchanged, rising and falling, rising and falling.

Danny returned to the crack and followed its course from start to end and back again while singing a verse from "*Tzur Mishelo*" under his breath.

His eye caught the window. It was a very large window, spanning the length of the wall. Light had begun to permeate the room, filling the window with a rich yellow-orange glow that drew Danny instantly from his bed. He rushed to the window and gasped at the most magnificent sight he had ever seen.

An endless expanse of land, totally void of any shape or form, stretched until as far as his eye could see. There was nothing except the earth and the horizon it melted into. Danny's old backyard, filled with garden tools, cleaning equipment, and garbage cans, had opened up into another backyard filled with garden tools, cleaning equipment, and garbage cans. He had never dreamed that one day his backyard would open up into a natural playground that shrugged off borders and burgeoned with possibilities that only the mind could limit.

Breathless, Danny studied the contours twisting and turning across the land, burrowing now and then into shapeless mounds, shooting off in every direction, splitting up and joining back again to form highways of lines, careening down the open freeway of ground. Imaginary cities sprouted up at the places of his choice. Tall, forest-clothed mountains swelled with railroad tracks hammered into the ground at lightning speed. Entire populations spread across the face of the land like dominoes. And just as quickly he could eliminate all of this with a sweep of his mental eraser across the blackboard of his dreams and build anew.

His mother entered the room.

"Mommy!" he cried excitedly, urging her to the window.

"Shhh." His mother stepped toward him, a finger on her lips. "What is it?"

"Look!" was all Danny could say.

"Yes, I see. It's very pretty."

Danny was silent, absorbed by the picture. His mother put her arm around him. "I'm glad you like it here." She gave him a squeeze and returned to her bed.

Danny continued to stare out the window. The light became stronger and the shadows smaller. The texture of the land became clearer. He imagined sitting there, playing with the soil. He could not wait to throw himself into it. Thoughts of his old home were forgotten for as long as he could keep his eyes frozen on the most beautiful field in the world.

2

"There's a problem with your coding," Ed, the project manager, remarked with a triumphant smirk.

Ezra Gelb had to fight, yet again, the urge to snap at his boss, who never passed up an opportunity to jab at him with his bitter needle. Ezra knew that some people carried baggage with them from a difficult childhood. He understood that when these people were placed in positions of power their insecurities manifested themselves in the form of intolerance or even mild totalitarianism. He realized that the Torah required him to swallow his pride and avoid reacting.

But every time an episode like this occurred, the reality of it caught him by surprise. Bubbles would boil somewhere deep inside him, and he would begin to froth at the mouth if he did not take immediate internal action to pop them. Afterward he would think, *I thought I had prepared myself for this...*

"Ed," Ezra responded, breathing out fumes through gritted teeth, "the program works. I've removed the bugs, and it's running just fine now. Why is the coding a problem if the program works?"

This little bit of defiance was just what Ed wanted to hear.

"Ezra, you need to review our policy," he said, his smirk still firmly in place. "Our company takes pride in its standards. And the standards are clean, efficient code, no matter what the program can do. A lot of people in the programming world are under this misconception that —"

"Ed, I..." The bubbles were churning and rising, and Alka-Seltzer would not do the trick.

It took a lot of painful determination, but Ezra managed to force a wave of calm to wash over him. Once it did, he knew he had won this battle, if not with Ed, then with another, defter creature that HaKadosh Baruch Hu in His great wisdom custom-designed inside each and every individual.

"That's a good point, Ed." The words lacked sincerity, but faking it was better than losing it. "What needs to be worked on in the code?"

"It's too lengthy, too clumsy. Uh, you know what I mean," Ed muttered with a flap of his wrist, as if to dismiss all of Ezra's work as hopeless, and then sauntered away to find another victim.

Ezra cupped his face in his hands and rubbed his eyes. Every time this happened it confirmed his secret decision to look for another job. In his mind he would bang his fist emphatically and say, "That does it!" The imaginary words would resound so loudly in his head that he would actually look over his shoulder to make sure no one had heard.

There were times when things weren't so bad, like when Ed was away and Ezra could work quietly on his own or another project manager would assign him tasks. At those times he would question his decision to leave, thinking that he did get a reasonable salary with fair benefits, and they allowed him to take off for the *chagim*. The job market was not exactly booming right now, and the thought of churning out a truckload of résumés, waiting with bated breath for the elusive "When can you start?" distressed him to the point of nauseating despondency.

But then, like an armored knight with a spiked tongue, Ed would appear and drive Ezra right back to his decision, prepared once again to abandon ship and forge ahead to new frontiers.

It wasn't as if he were married to the company. If you could bow out of a business situation without stepping on anyone's toes, there was no reason to stay there.

As it turned out, he had an interview scheduled to take place in two hours. Just the thought of it made him straighten his tie and clear his throat. He had been at this company for three years, and the whole interview process had been shoved to the recesses of his mind. Now he had to familiarize himself with it again. He swallowed hard. It irked him that he was nervous. He reminded himself that everything was in Hashem's hands. It was all a matter of *bitachon*.

He had spent hours discussing the subject of *bitachon* with his friend, Aryeh, at the dining-room table in Aryeh's home over countless glasses of seltzer and endless mounds of cookies. Ezra's interest in the subject was not purely academic. He and Devorah had been married for four years, and they had no children. Most couples in their position would experience tension and become depressed, with the wife experiencing these feelings more intensely. In the case of Ezra and Devorah, it was different.

Not that Devorah was apathetic. On the contrary, she was one of the most sensitive people Ezra had ever known. But she displayed an iron-clad level of *bitachon* that, on the one hand, inspired Ezra and made him grateful for having being provided with such a life partner and, on the other, intimidated him and sent chills of fear down his spine when he considered the daunting task of aspiring to her level.

Ever since she had discovered her roots and during her early years at seminary in Yerushalayim, she had acquired an unshakable faith in HaKadosh Baruch Hu. For her it was natural and so obvious. *Of course* everything God did in the world was for the good. He created it. He continued to create it anew every moment. How could one think for a minute that God was not in control?

Ezra understood this intellectually, but, like most people, it was one thing to talk about it, another thing to feel it. There was a long way from the head to the heart. Either Devorah had found a shortcut, or she was quite capable of traveling the distance.

Aryeh would plead with Ezra to find a *rav* with whom to speak about these very important issues. Ezra would respond that he had made some effort in this regard, but the people with whom he felt he could really connect were usually the ones with such hectic schedules that they could hardly breathe, let alone answer Ezra's calls. If only there were someone right here in Grandridge whom he could turn to. But that was like hoping for real diamonds in a packet of party favors.

Ezra stared at his computer screen. With a sigh, he got back to work on refining his code. He took off his watch and placed it next to the screen. He glanced now and then at the minutes ticking away toward the interview.

The secretary buzzed him.

"There's someone here to see you, Mr. Gelb."

"Okay. I'll be right out."

In the lobby stood a woman, one hand on the reception desk and the other waving at the passersby like she was their mother.

"Ima!" Ezra exclaimed. He put a smile on his face as he strode up to his mother. She hardly ever came to the office unannounced.

"Hello, my sweetheart." Her hand reached up to stroke her tall son's face.

"Is everything all right, Ima?"

"Oh, everything is fine. I was just at the store getting some fish. The salmon is on sale for a quarter of the price. I thought I should take advantage of it, especially since Abba likes it so much, although you know he won't eat it unless I bake it with a ton of garlic. You know how much he likes garlic. You kids never liked it much, and you would always make me scrape off the garlic. *Oy!*" she gasped, clasping her hand over mouth. "I don't think I have enough garlic! And I was just at the store. Now why didn't I think of it when I was there? I was right by the vegetables. I think I even bought a couple of tomatoes, which were probably right next to the garlic."

Her hand dove into the plastic bag that hung from the crook of her elbow to confirm her misfortune. "Yes, I bought tomatoes. I can't believe it. Aah!" The palm of her hand knocked against her forehead. "I'm getting old, Benny…"

"Ezra."

"I mean Ezra. You see what I mean?"

They both chuckled.

"So...Ima," Ezra said, folding his hands and smiling patiently, "how...er...what..."

"Oh, yes," she said, patting his wrist. "While I was at the store, I thought I would pick you up a little *pekele*, a little candy, some crackers, you know, so you can take it with you to your..." Her voiced lowered to a whisper, her eyes bulging with the urgency of the highly classified tidbit.

They both mouthed the word *interview*.

Ezra, his face pink, muttered a "thank you." Looking slowly to the left and then to the right, his mother handed him the goods.

"*Oy!*" she sighed, relieved that the transaction was complete and had gone undetected. "What can I say, sweetheart? I wish you lots of *berachah*. I'm thinking of you. Now I have to go to the bank before it closes because they haven't sent the whatchamacallit — the statement Abba asked them for. And the dry cleaner is closing early today because he's flying out to his daughter's wedding, but I need my suit for what's-his-name's bar mitzvah this Shabbos. Actually, I don't remember which suit I gave him — was it the lavender one with the thing on the side or the long blue one? I thought the blue one was hanging in the other closet by the wall." She stopped to contemplate this, her thumb brushing her bottom lip.

"Ima, I have to go. Thank you so much..."

"Oh, I hope it's enough for you," she said, eyeing the bag in his hand. "Maybe I should have gotten you some fruit to give you energy. It's much healthier."

"Don't worry, Ima. I'm sure I'll be fine."

She waved goodbye and headed for the elevator, stopping to chat with one or two employees whom Ezra himself had never even greeted before.

🌿 🌿 🌿

"I'm looking at your résumé now," Kevin, a young man in his late twenties, stated with a repulsive smugness, his head swinging back and forth like a pendulum as he scanned Ezra's details. A pen dangled from the corner of his mouth and was flipped up and down at the end of every paragraph he read.

This was surely another challenge — being interviewed by someone younger than him and, even more difficult, someone younger than him who purported to be his senior.

"Hmmm," Kevin murmured, the pen still dangling. His hair stood straight up in a heavily greased style that resembled the perfectly aligned stalks of a wheat field. He looked up at Ezra with a curious stare, finally removing the pen.

"Why did you drop out of medical school, Ezra?" Kevin inquired in a tone that could not be mistaken for anything but pure condescension.

Ezra's résumé did mention this particular fact, though certainly not in such crude terms. It would take a Kevin to translate it into more offensive terminology.

"I found that it was taking up my whole life — there was so

much work. Now, I do believe in hard work, but at the same time I believe in time spent with family and –" he wanted to say "Torah study" but decided to be more general "– and time for other pursuits."

"What are those other pursuits?"

Ezra shifted in his chair. "Just, you know, doing chores and...and volunteer work." He smiled, knowing that this should impress an employer.

Kevin's eyes seemed to dart now and then to the top of Ezra's head, where the velvet beast lay, its claws embedded in the thick of Ezra's hair. Although Kevin hadn't said anything in particular that could nail him as prejudiced, it usually wasn't difficult to detect it.

Then Ezra was struck by another sneaking suspicion. He boldly threw out the question.

"Kevin, are you Jewish, by any chance?"

Kevin's jaw dropped ever so slightly. "Yes, I am. Why do you ask?" Now it was his turn to shift in his chair.

Ezra smiled to himself. "Oh, just curious." How predictable. For most of his non-Jewish business colleagues, his *kippah* was at the most a mild subject of interest, and even then it was purely academic. For many of his Jewish colleagues, however, the *kippah* was a formidable threat, ranging from a mere yellow alert to a full-on code-red emergency.

"Are we going to talk about computers today?" Ezra quipped, capitalizing on his own brazenness and Kevin's momentary fall from grandeur.

The young interviewer shuffled his notes and returned to his former posture. He began quizzing Ezra on his programming knowledge and experience. It was not long before that inimitable pen found its way back to the corner of his mouth, flipping up and down like a robotic arm.

*   *   *

The day was not over. After *ma'ariv*, tired as he was, Ezra had a meeting to attend. The Ohr Yisrael Shul had convened yet another board meeting to discuss the gnawing, ever-present financial crisis. Tonight they would, once again, brainstorm for a successful, innovative fund-raising strategy. One would have imagined this to be a stimulating, creative experience, where eager minds met to whip up a storm of exciting ideas.

One would have been wrong.

The problem, Ezra had diagnosed, after many months of protracted discourse of which he was more a spectator than a participant, was that people had a tendency to express their opinions. Nothing wrong with that. But the trouble was that people also had a tendency not to listen to other people's opinions. Now that presented quite a problem, because opinions were being dispensed like birdseed in Trafalgar Square, and no pigeons were swooping down to eat them. In fact, a whole heap of opinions lay on the table in front of them, piled up and left there to decay over the years. This meant, Ezra surmised, that the only way unanimous agreement would be reached was if everyone on the board would think of the same brilliant idea at the very same time, the possibility of which was obviously extremely remote.

Many times he had felt the urge to rebuke his *chaveirim*. Certainly this was not the way of the Torah. But he wasn't sure if he could do so out of pure love and concern for his fellow Jews, a precondition for rebuke. He wasn't sure his rebuke would be totally altruistic. Selfish motivations were always prime suspects in cases like these.

"I don't think that's going to work," Mike said, grimacing at a suggestion made by Arthur.

"Why not?" Arthur challenged.

"It's too..." Mike made a dismissive gesture.

"It's too what?" Arthur persisted.

"I don't know. I just don't think it's going to work."

Of course, Arthur was not exactly elated with this line of reasoning, or lack thereof.

"You can't just say you don't like it without telling me why!" Arthur exclaimed. He turned to the rest of the assembly and said excitedly, "You see, this is why the —"

"I'll tell you why. I'll tell you why!" Mike interrupted, having thought of a reason at the last moment. He proceeded to deliver a very well-calculated critique of Arthur's suggestion that would take a chunk out of every bone and fiber of Arthur's argument.

A brief pause followed.

"I don't agree with you," Arthur declared defiantly.

Ezra rolled his eyes. As long as this meeting wasn't going anywhere, his mind could drift to the image of the Jewish kid, Kevin, perhaps his future boss. Was it wise to even contemplate moving to a company where a guy like Kevin would be giving him the orders?

Was there any reason to believe that working for Kevin would be better than working for Ed?

It was difficult to know how he had fared at the end of the interview. Kevin did not let on. He merely closed the proceedings with a mechanical "We'll contact you" and "That's all for now."

The shul meeting finally came to a conclusion with at least one decision that everyone agreed upon: there was a need to schedule another meeting to discuss this further.

Ezra closed his shul file, packed it in his briefcase, and trudged out the door to his car. At last he was going home.

He always looked forward to his wife's smile as he came in the door. He spent the drive home imagining what her day was like. She was as busy as he, running from one activity to another. She worked as a secretary for Ohr Yisrael in the mornings, volunteered as an English teacher in a nearby settlement for Russian Jewish immigrants in the afternoons three times a week, ran a tape *gemach* from their home, and was, of course, his devoted *eishes chayil*. It wasn't like they never argued, over issues varying from daily ("and I mean daily") garbage removal to finances ("I thought we agreed not to spend any money on that"). But on the whole things were good.

When Ezra walked in the door, she was standing right there, standing so very still. It seemed as if she had been waiting there for hours. Her eyes were puffy and her smile faltering.

"What happened?" Ezra stammered, rushing inside.

"Oh, Ezra, I'm sorry I gave you a fright. Nothing's wrong. Really."

He inspected her again. He noticed her hand was gripping a *Tehillim*.

"Come on, Devorah. Please tell me."

A peculiar smile spread over her face. She beckoned him to the dining room. The table was set in Shabbos finery. A beautiful bouquet of fresh flowers sprouted up from the center of the table and hung gracefully over the gold-rimmed china, the sparkling cutlery, and the gleaming wine glasses.

What on earth was going on?

She showed him to his seat and sat down in hers all without a word. Then she pointed to a small gold jewelry box tied with ribbon. His mind quickly did a date search — birthday, wedding anniversary, engagement anniversary. Search results: zero.

He untied the ribbon and opened the box. Inside was a thin piece of paper with just a few words.

I took a little test this morning.

Ezra looked up at his wife. Her eyes were filled with tears. "HaKadosh Baruch Hu has answered our prayers," she uttered haltingly, hardly believing the words that were coming out of her mouth.

He was riveted to the spot. A wave of sublime joy crashed over him, almost throwing him to the ground. Thoughts of Ed and his interview evaporated instantly. It was the most beautiful moment in the world.

3

Plowing

Yosef thrashed around excitedly in the playpen (the crib hadn't been set up yet). Danny followed his mother around as she hunted for a missing baby sock, opening and shutting this box, that drawer.

"When are we going, Mommy?" At this point, Danny's whine sounded like the hinges of a rusted door.

"Soon, Danny. I have to find Yosef's sock and then we can (closet door slams) go."

"Oh."

Yosef was beginning to whimper.

"Is this it?" Danny held up a sock like a fish he had caught on an expedition.

His mother spun around and shook her head in disbelief. "Danny, where was that?"

"Next to the diapers."

In a flash, the baby was ready and strapped in his stroller. They stepped out the door into the fresh country air. Fresh did not necessarily mean pleasant, though.

"Eww! What's that smell?" Danny scrunched up his nose.

"It's manure," his mother informed him and then proceeded to expound, to the best of her knowledge, on the more rudimentary habits of animals.

They made their way by foot to the only kosher bakery in town, a pleasant twenty-minute walk down the main street, which started a mere couple of blocks ahead of them.

"Do the animals eat you?" Danny asked.

"No, no, not these animals. If you were in the jungle, maybe you would have to worry, but not here. Come, hold my hand. We have to cross this street."

Danny was on the lookout at every approaching corner for an animal waiting to jump out and pounce on him, scoop him up neatly in its paws, and start munching on his arm like it was a candy bar. He touched his arm, anticipating the impending pain.

They entered the bakery and were immediately enveloped by that incomparable fresh bread and cake smell. Danny forgot his arm for the moment and raced up to the glass display that held the cookies. An enticing variety of shapes and colors paraded in front of his eyes.

A smiling face suddenly appeared on the other side of the glass, between the chocolate fudge and the apple crumble. Then the man behind the counter stood up straight and peered over the edge to look down upon the boy.

"Hi, there, young man. Haven't seen you in here before."

Danny stepped back shyly, almost bumping into the bagel stand. His hands flitted in the direction of his mother, though his eyes remained fixed on this chubby man with the short gray moustache.

"What's your name?"

A finger went into his mouth.

"Is it Moshe? Yaakov?"

A widening smile.

"Is it Teddy Bear? Toy Car?"

Danny giggled, his finger still wedged in his mouth. His mother was flipping through some cookbooks at the other end of the store.

"It's Danny," he murmured.

"Danny! What a great name. So let me guess your Hebrew name. Daniel ben…"

"No, no," Danny interrupted. "It's Daniel Eliezer ben Menachem."

"Oh, excuse me," the baker said.

Danny's mother came up to the counter and introduced herself. While the adults launched into their more sedate mode of communication, which to Danny was a drone akin to that of distant freeway traffic, he roamed around the store, glancing every now and then at the chubby man with the short gray moustache. He was fascinated by the way the moustache bounced up and down every time the man spoke. The man laughed at something he himself had said. It was a loud, booming laugh that almost rattled the shelves. Danny giggled again.

Finally his mother concluded her purchases. She handed him a small parcel to carry and tucked another in the basket underneath the stroller. Then she grabbed Danny's hand, and they made their way out the door, Danny's head swiveling in the direction of the baker who was now cleaning the counter.

"Mommy, who's that?"

"That's the baker."

"What does he do?"

"He makes bread. Hold my hand. We're going to cross the street."

They scurried across the street even though there were no cars to be seen.

"But you said that Hashem makes bread."

Rachel smiled. This was one of those big questions she had always pictured would surface on a leisurely winter evening over a cup of cocoa and a bedtime story. Instead they usually cropped up in the thick of errands and activity, on a main downtown street, when Yosef was acting up, as he was now, and she had to rush home to deal with a mountain of laundry and dishes.

"You're right, Danny. Very good. Hashem made the whole world. But He gives us the chance to use what He created to..." Yosef's bottle fell to the ground. She crouched to pick it up and returned it to him. "You see, He wants us to use everything and make things from it. So the baker uses what he needs to make bread, but without Hashem He wouldn't have anything to make it from. And in any case, without Hashem there wouldn't even be a baker or you or me."

She could see Danny was trying to process the information, although she knew even for adults it was not easy to comprehend these ideas. She herself had a hard time with it. Surely the finished product, too, was a creation of Hashem. Somehow she understood this to be true, although it was difficult to articulate to herself or anyone else exactly how it worked.

※ ※ ※

Yosef was still crying when they got back to the house. Danny ran inside and scaled the staircase within seconds and then bolted down again in even shorter time. This had become his regular declaration of arrival in his new house.

"Danny, please be careful," Rachel warned limply, knowing her words were futile. She knew he needed to be back in school, where his reservoir of energy would be usefully channeled. They were planning to enroll him soon in a small cheder that was located in a town closer to the city. But for now his energy was spilling everywhere.

"Why don't you go play outside in the backyard?" She took Yosef out of the stroller and sat down to nurse him.

Danny's eyes lit up. The backyard was still uncharted territory.

He walked cautiously out the back door into the yard. It was a small area of mostly sand and patches of yellowing grass. His little scooter had already been unpacked and was waiting for him in the shade of the oak tree. The yard was enclosed by an old, warped chain-link fence clutching each end of the house for support. But the fence did not interest him, nor did his scooter. It was what lay beyond the fence and the scooter that intrigued him, that which his eyes had beheld the other morning, that which he had begun to doubt as being real.

Perhaps it had been a dream. Only the night before he had dreamed that he was back in his old house, staring at his *Krias Shema* poster and playing with his carrot-colored teddy bear with the narrow black currant eyes. But here was this magnificent field sprawled in front of him, stretching to the horizon. He smelled the raw freshness of the soil and the grass and the cool breeze that brushed it and washed over him. He needed to be there. He walked up to the fence and poked his fingers through the rusted mesh, pressing his face as far up against the wire as he could.

He could not hold back. His heart pounding, he glanced behind him at the house. Through the window he could see his mother moving around in the kitchen. Carefully he inserted his sneaker into a little pocket in the mesh and lifted himself up. The fence began to sway and buckle, so he moved faster, bringing his left leg up and swinging himself over to the other side. He tried to get a foothold going down but he couldn't find a pocket in the mesh quickly enough. The fence buckled and threw him to the ground. He muffled his cries as he landed in a dust cloud. Looking quickly up at the window through the dust, now from the other side of the fence, he saw his mother still moving around in the kitchen undisturbed.

Slowly he turned around and faced the field. He stood up and began treading the soil, a mischievous smile lighting his dust-plastered face. He moved faster, watching how his feet pressed prints into the soil. Then faster, until he was sprinting at full speed, his chest puffed out and his arms flailing. He was laughing and trying to breathe at the same time, soaking in the air and blowing it out, as he sped toward the horizon. Eventually he became too tired to continue and purposely collapsed in a heap, giggling and gasping for breath.

He looked back and saw his house in the distance. He was too far away to see if his mother had noticed him gone. He would rest there in the soil until he had recovered. Not completely, though. Just enough to be able to breathe while he continued to sprint.

🌿 🌿 🌿

If there ever was a stigma to being the new kid in school, Danny was feeling it in all its miserable glory. In a small town, where the number of *frum* kids never exceeded the number of classrooms in the building, the tendency toward xenophobia was more pronounced then ever. They were good kids. But kids would be kids, and whatever the *yetzer hara* insisted on would generally turn out to be the order of the day. They stared at him, whispered and giggled among themselves, and halted all activity at once when Danny opened his mouth to speak, as if he were a Martian trying to blend in with the earthlings.

It was no surprise, then, that when Danny's mother came to pick him up on the first day, she found him sitting downcast on the grass just inside the school gate.

"Danny, what's wrong?" She gave him a hug. He didn't answer, but he really didn't have to. She had figured it out. She and

Menachem had expected something like this. She would have to talk to his rebbe.

"Danny, do you like your new rebbe?" she asked as she finished buckling him in.

Danny remained silent. She got inside the car and drove toward the freeway. *Oy*, the guilt. Guilt was an integral part of her being. It seemed she had been naturally endowed with an inordinate propensity for it, even for a Jewish mother. What had she done to her poor son? He had adored Rabbi Menkin, and Rabbi Menkin had adored him. And she had snatched him away for her own selfish considerations. Though it had been a joint decision with Menachem, it was really she who had insisted on the move, she who had needed an improvement in their financial situation.

Oy, the guilt. What had she done to her poor husband? There were visions of her seminary teacher espousing the virtues of *deveikus*, a sublime clinging to Hashem, overcoming any obsession with the material as the be-all and end-all, and here she was dragging her family to the treasure-trove of Grandridge.

Inside the house, she thought she'd console her son with a little sweet. "Danny, Mommy wants to give you a treat. What can I give you, sweetheart?"

He looked up at her. "I want to go play outside."

Rachel smiled. "Okay." She gave him a kiss, and he rushed out the back door. She turned to the stack of boxes in the living room and, with a sigh, began to tackle them.

Danny scanned the kitchen window. There was no one there. He sneaked up to the fence and searched for the pocket in the mesh. With little effort he was able to scale the fence, jumping from the top instead of trying to get a foothold on the other side. He relished the sudden sense of freedom, all borders swept aside.

Today he was Moshe Rabbeinu, leading the throngs of Jewish people through the desert under the harsh sun. A tiny mound in the far corner of his eye swelled suddenly into a mountain that he would ascend to bring down the Torah just liked Rabbi Menkin had taught. He rushed toward the mountain and stopped short of it. He turned to face the multitude of people and raised his hand.

"Stop!" he commanded. "You, too! Stop!" he admonished a three-year-old who was trying to push to the front line.

"Now," he continued, "Hashem is going to give us the Torah. I want everyone to sing along with me. 'Torah, Torah, Torah...Torah, Torah, Torah...Torah tzivah lanu Moshe.'" A deafening roar of impassioned voices sang in unison in a way that would have made Uncle Moishy proud.

Danny pranced around the foot of the mountain, spurring everyone on. Suddenly a very real noise rocked the quiet cool air behind him. He froze. The mountain shriveled up, and the people vanished. He was alone with something on the field. Something in the distance was powering its way toward him, crackling and rumbling, gaining momentum.

Danny instinctively took a step backward and stumbled to the ground. He stared at this ominous shadow as its form bulged and lapped up the earth. A ruffled haze encompassed it. As it got closer, Danny could see chunks of soil flying in the air. Whatever it was, it appeared to be eating the soil.

His heart leaped. The fear that had seized him made him immobile, pinning him in this extremely vulnerable position to the ground. In the last few weeks, he had dreamed of the animals his mother had spoken about, chasing him and cornering him, and in the dreams he had been unable to move. It seemed now that he was dreaming, too — or was he?

With all his strength, he jumped to his feet, and at once he knew it wasn't a dream, because he could run. He ran with all his might, kicking up a storm of dirt in his path, zeroing in on the fence. Tears streamed down his face but were instantly wiped away by the stinging wind.

Without daring to look back, he scrambled recklessly up the wire. As he pushed himself over, his leg caught on a stray barb, and it ripped through his pants to his skin. He shrieked in pain, but was cut short by the resounding thud of his landing on the gravelly ground, wrist first.

*   *   *

Dr. Jenson was curious to know what neat little trick was the instigator in this, the latest of countless similar injuries he had seen in boys this age.

"Don't even ask," Rachel replied wryly.

The doctor smiled as he put the finishing touches to Danny's cast. He then proceeded to give instructions to his mother on maneuvering the sling and cleaning the surrounding area. After that came the tetanus shot. Danny winced even as he saw the spiraling spike of the needle being prepared.

He put on a brave face throughout. But in the car, on the freeway, he burst into tears. Rachel quickly pulled over to the side. "What's the matter, sweetheart?" she asked frantically from the front seat. She was afraid to get out, since the cars were whizzing past them, lifting the car slightly with their force.

Danny could not talk. All he could do was cry.

"Is it your arm?"

Danny shook his head.

"Your leg? Does the injection hurt?"

Once again he shook his head.

She stared at him helplessly. "Mommy will hold you when we get home, okay?"

She sped back onto the freeway, and Yosef, of course, began to voice his appeal to be replenished in the food department so that a veritable wailing symphony accompanied her back to their new, still unsettled home.

After she nursed Yosef and put him down to sleep, she picked up Danny, who lay curled on the couch, his pale white cast resting heavily over his waist. She held him in the rocking chair, settling him awkwardly in her lap. They sat quietly, only the rhythmic creaking of the chair echoing through the room.

She thought about calling Menachem to tell him how it had gone at the doctor. She glanced at her watch. He would be in a meeting for at least another thirty minutes.

"Mommy?"

"Yes, Danny."

"Did you see the monster?"

She frowned. Then it dawned on her that he must be referring to the tractor he had been running from in the field.

"Danny, it wasn't a monster. It was just a tractor. Do you know what a tractor is?"

Danny shook his head. "It was a monster," he said with greater conviction.

She stroked his hair and continued to rock him. It would be difficult to convince him of anything right now.

🌿 🌿 🌿

Danny's eyes popped open as the first rays of sunlight streamed into his room. The monster disappeared, after having enveloped him in a crushing squeeze from which he could not escape. Its metal claws had sunk deep into his flesh. Now the searing pain they had caused also disappeared.

He listened for other sounds. He heard only the familiar rhythm of breathing as his family slept. Afraid to close his eyes again, he pulled himself up and out of bed and padded over to the window. He stood in the partition of the curtains where the light filtered through. The vast field met his eyes again, bathed in the soft glow of the morning light.

He strained his eyes to study the soil and swallowed hard. He had been right. Instead of a giant, flat, untouched bed of earth, there were now dents and grooves and patches of chewed-up soil.

His magnificent playground had been reduced to a mass of shredded earth. The monster had done this.

Where was the monster now? He darted back to his bed and pulled the covers up to his eyes.

4

Several months and a number of hushed-up rendezvous later, Ezra was offered the job. It happened on a cold, damp morning on what Ezra thought was another mere brown-bag excursion to their offices to meet yet another department manager. This time, however, it was the original viceroy, Kevin, who greeted him with a fraction of a smile and ushered him into his office for a formal offer of employment.

Ezra was taken aback. "Oh" was all he could say.

Kevin's pen was still flicking up and down like a dragon's forked tongue. Ezra was trying to visualize how he would incinerate that pen one day while Kevin wasn't looking, although this would not exactly be following in the way of piety.

After a little salary game of chess, which Ezra won, he heaved a great sigh and signed on the dotted line.

Now that he had been inaugurated, it seemed natural to lower the conversation to small talk, an involuntary, teeth-gritting opportunity to "get to know each other." It turned out that Kevin's father was a primary shareholder in the company, and it was he who got Kevin the job as human resources director. No surprises there.

Kevin wasn't married and declared that marriage was "an institution imposed upon normal society by religious strictures," a declaration Ezra duly ignored. *Wait until he meets his future wife,* Ezra thought. *She'll make him eat his words.* Maybe it was this remark, or maybe it was a number of other subtle messages Kevin evinced, but Ezra got the sense that not all was rosy in the life of this valiant young upstart. He would modify his attitude toward Kevin from one of defense to one of sympathy. Perhaps here was a chance to help a fellow Jew.

*   *   *

How it happened that Ezra was able to get Kevin to come for Shabbos, Ezra could not fathom. One Friday a group of guys at the office had been discussing their plans for the weekend. It seemed Kevin was undecided, and Ezra had flippantly suggested that he might enjoy experiencing a Shabbos. He was surprised when Kevin accepted, albeit with a casual "Yeah, sure," as if he were agreeing to a movie and popcorn. It appeared that his superior's reservations about religious Jews had been put aside for the moment.

So here he was, seated next to Abba. Abba and Ima always came for Shabbos, unless they were traveling somewhere on a kosher cruise. Two weeks before each cruise, Ima would not stop talking about the craziness of the itinerary, the menu, and the detailed weather forecasts for each port. Two weeks after the cruise, she would not stop talking about the craziness of the itinerary, the menu, and the detailed weather accounts of each port.

"I mean, have you ever? They said there would be a zero percent chance of rain."

"Not zero percent," Abba chimed in.

"I'm telling you, I heard him say zero percent. He even said it with that smile of his, you know, that 'I'm always right' thing that he does."

Devorah chuckled as she passed a plate of chopped liver to Kevin. No one noticed how Kevin's eyes lit up as he stared at a dish he was last served when he was a child.

"And then we're standing there in the pouring rain, and the guide is pointing to a mountain we can't see because it's raining, and he just goes on talking about it for half an hour..."

"It wasn't half an hour," Abba intervened.

"Well, it felt like it. It felt like an hour, actually. Why couldn't we have just stayed inside, and he could have shown us a picture of it or something?"

"Because it wouldn't have been worth the money you paid for it, Ima," Benny retorted playfully.

Benny was Ezra's brother. He and his wife and kids were there for the Friday night meal.

"Oh, worth the money!" she exclaimed through a mouthful of salad. "You should have seen how expensive it was to order a simple drink."

"Whiskey?" Benny teased.

"No, not whiskey." She flapped her hand at him. "Just a soda. And then they pile it up with blocks of ice so you have to go looking for the soda between the ice. Everything today is a marketing gimmick. They always say to me, 'Is there anything else I can help you with today, Mrs. Gelb?' You think they really want to help me?

They want to help me just as much as Frank, that car salesman, wants to help me when he keeps calling me. He says I could get a good price for my car when I trade it in, and that I'd be making an investment by buying a new one. Well, there's nothing wrong with my car right now as it is. I mean, it does need something new according to your Abba. What was it again, Abe?"

"An engine," Benny quipped.

Everyone at the table chuckled, including Kevin, who had been quietly observing the scene. Mingled with the talking was the clattering of plates, the clinking of wine glasses, and the intermittent shrieks of the children, who had transformed the dining area into a perilous obstacle course. Still, there was something so profoundly calming amid all this commotion, something that contrasted starkly to his TV dinner and beer or his usual trip to a nightclub that pulled him through Friday nights.

When Devorah sank into her chair with a plate of liver and a relieved smile, it dawned on everyone that they hadn't been helping her as much as they should have.

"*Oy*, what kind of mother-in-law am I anyway!" Ezra's mother chided herself as she rose to clear some dishes, although Devorah, of course, raised her hand to refuse any advances. A friendly little battle ensued, as it did most Friday nights, about whether or not Devorah needed any help. Ezra would smile at such a worthwhile dispute, and right in the middle of this spirited din, he would launch into Shabbos *zemiros*, which would fan the warm flames of all this clamor, so that on this particular occasion Kevin would learn that there existed such a thing as beautiful noise.

Ezra returned from another teeth-pulling meeting at shul. At least tonight they had committed, on paper, to a fund-raising strategy that the majority of the board agreed upon. The only problem was that the actual strategy itself was going to cost money to implement, and the board would have to meet again to decide where that money was going to come from.

Devorah had tea ready for him when he walked in the door. She looked a little weary from standing much of the day.

"How are you feeling?" he asked her before unloading the events of his own hectic day.

She smiled. "*Baruch Hashem*. Just rolling along. I have some sores in my mouth, though. I think I may be getting a cold."

"How many days do you have left at the shul office?"

"Well..." She counted on her fingers. "About nine."

"Maybe you can ask for leave a little earlier. It's too stressful for you."

"Maybe." She shrugged. "We'll see how I feel tomorrow."

The next day he was staring blankly at his screen, trying to figure out why a particular bug in the program just wouldn't go away. The secretary buzzed. "It's your wife, Mr. Gelb."

Devorah told him that her entire mouth hurt although she displayed no symptoms of a cold. She had left work in the morning and made a visit to the doctor. He had suggested that her wisdom teeth were infecting her mouth and that they should be surgically removed.

Ezra sat back in his chair. "Is that a common thing?"

"I don't know. He didn't seem to know the cause of the infection, but, of course, he did tell me how common it is to have one's wisdom teeth removed."

"But what about the fact that you're pregnant?"

"Right. So he said that surgery is risky, and I should really wait until after I've given birth, since I'm in my thirty-fifth week anyway. In the meantime, he's prescribed antibiotics that are safe to take during pregnancy."

Ezra leaned forward and tapped his fingers on his desk. They were both silent for a while. There was an almost tangible undercurrent of nervousness.

"So are you calling from home or from work?" he asked finally.

"From work. Apart from my mouth, I feel all right. Just a little tired. I've already gotten my prescription filled, and I've taken my first dose."

"Is it painful to talk?"

"A little."

"A little" in Devorah's vocabulary usually translated as "A lot, but I'm dealing with it."

He told her to get into bed the minute she got home, and he would be there as soon as he could. He would throw together some food for dinner, perhaps call Ima to come over and help, but he didn't want to worry her.

Devorah's parents were out of town, and in any case their

relationship with their daughter was strained. They had never come to terms with her decision to become more observant, despite countless overtures on Devorah's part to convince them that nothing had changed in how she felt about them. On the contrary, she would point out, her new lifestyle had deepened her appreciation of her parents and what they had done for her. But they closed their ears to her entreaties. Any attempt at reconciliation was defiantly and abruptly halted with a crude and painful remark that Devorah would bravely deflect. Still, she tried to keep the lines of communication open, even if it meant making herself into an open target.

Ezra turned his attention to the computer screen and chewed on his knuckles. The jumble of code stared up at him, waiting for him to continue. It was going to be really difficult to concentrate now. He remembered a *devar Torah* he had heard at a Shabbos table about what made a person great. The real trick in life was the ability to focus on the moment at hand. The great tzaddikim would pour every ounce of energy they had into what Hashem required of them at each moment. That was the secret of success in Torah learning, in *tefillah*, in empathizing with a fellow Jew, in all areas of life. To be able to block out all else was an art. And it took many years of hard work to cultivate it.

With a sigh, he returned to his work.

🌿 🌿 🌿

Devorah greeted Ezra with her usual smile when he walked in. She was wiping the table, trying awkwardly to reach the far points from where she stood.

He shook his head at her. "Devorah, you're supposed to be in bed."

"I was in bed. I lay there for hours. I read a little, slept a little. And then I had enough."

Ezra laughed. He wasn't going to change his wife.

It turned out she had actually made a little something for dinner — steaming lasagna with a potpourri of vegetables to accompany it. That was all.

"Have you taken your second dose yet?"

"Oh, thanks for reminding me. I'm supposed to take it before meals." Devorah excused herself.

Ezra was about to dig into his lasagna when she appeared suddenly in the doorway. She stood very still, her face pale. He dropped his fork.

"Ezra, I think there's something very wrong."

※ ※ ※

They stared at each other wordlessly during the ambulance ride. The paramedic asked Devorah a number of questions as he treated her. Mostly her answer was no. She did not feel the onset of labor. She felt no abdominal pain.

"I forgot to bring a *Tehillim*," Ezra said to her finally, clearing his throat, as she was wheeled up to the prenatal ward.

"There's one in my purse."

Within minutes she was attached to a fetal monitor, and the sound of a steady heartbeat reverberated through the room. She was hooked up to an IV, and two physicians were standing at the entrance to the room discussing something. Ezra and Devorah were quiet, watching all of this activity taking place around them, feeling like spectators even though they were the main attraction.

The curtains around Devorah were drawn, and Ezra was pushed out of the way with a curt "Excuse me." He took a deep breath and reached for the *Tehillim* inside Devorah's purse. He found a chair and sat down, opened the *sefer* at random, and began to recite, injecting such force into the words it took him by surprise. It seemed as if the energy was tangible, in such close proximity, allowing access to it with the slightest of ease. He was instantly soaring with the poetic majesty of King David's words.

Eventually the curtains opened, and the doctors emerged, followed by the nurses. The doctors were still engaged in conversation, but everyone looked more relaxed.

A doctor made his way over to Ezra, who closed his *Tehillim* and jumped to his feet.

"Mr. Gelb, I'm Dr. Jeremy Michaels." He extended a hand, a loose fringe of hair flapping over his forehead as he did so. He was even smiling.

"Hi," Ezra replied meekly.

"Well, it looks like the baby is doing just fine."

Ezra breathed a sigh of relief.

"There is no sign of fetal distress. The baby is active, and the heartbeat is strong and regular. We'll keep your wife here overnight just to make sure, and then she will be free to go home." He ended off the sentence with an almost melodic twist, as a way of wholeheartedly endorsing his prognosis. "Just make sure she stays off her feet until the end of the pregnancy," he added.

"But what was wrong? What caused it?" Ezra persisted.

"Well, it could be a number of factors, some of them serious, some not. Usually it's because the mother is not resting enough. Your wife told me that she is still working. I told her that should really stop."

Ezra nodded. The doctor turned to leave.

But Ezra wouldn't let go. "But it might happen again?"

"Well," the doctor responded, in a slightly less cheerful tone, "maybe. But since the baby is doing just fine and there are no other problems, it seems there is nothing to worry about. All right?" He patted Ezra's shoulder in that pretentiously chummy way. Ezra did not answer, but the doctor didn't wait for him anyway.

Only one nurse remained in the room now. She was busily jotting something down on the chart at the foot of Devorah's bed. Ezra went over to Devorah's bedside.

"Well, it seems everything's fine," he said, shrugging his shoulders. Devorah gave him a blank stare. Neither was totally convinced.

Ezra looked at the animated fetal monitor, which blinked and punched out sounds, methodically sketching a continuous graph on paper that it spewed out. The baby did sound fine. Maybe they were being paranoid.

He looked at his watch. "Wow! Do you realize it's after midnight?"

Devorah raised her eyebrows.

He was suddenly tired and hungry. Looking at his watch had

brought him back down to his corporeal routine.

"Do you want me to go home and bring that lasagna?" he proposed.

She chuckled. "The hospital food is probably better than my food."

"Yeah, right. There are some things I'm pretty sure of. And this is one of them."

🌿 🌿 🌿

Somehow Ima had found out, because she was at Devorah's bedside early the next morning. Ezra awoke in the chair by the window to find her standing with her feet together, her purse hanging from the crook of her arm, peering over Devorah's sleeping face with a look of sheer angst.

"Ima!" he croaked.

"Shhh! Don't wake her. She needs to rest." She stalked over to Ezra.

"Ima, how did you find out?"

"I called you late last night because I wanted to ask Devorah for her apple crumble recipe. She puts something in it that gives it that extra oomph, and I can't figure out what it is. Abba thinks it's pepper, have you ever heard? No wonder I don't let him anywhere near the kitchen. Anyway, I called and there was no answer. So I figured maybe you'd gone out for coffee or something. But then I remembered that the kosher coffee shop closes early. I don't understand them — it's like they don't want to make money or something. Sometimes you just want a coffee late at night, you know what I mean? And they close so early." She shook her head. "Anyway, I called again later. Abba thought I was meshugah, but by now it was midnight and there was still no answer. So I thought, well, she's almost thirty-six weeks, you know. So I called the hospital, and they told me she was here. I got all excited, but then they told me she wasn't in the labor ward, she was in the prenasal ward..."

"Prenatal."

"Prenatal. Whatever. *Oy*, I got so scared. But then I spoke to a wonderful young doctor – Dr. Michaels?"

Ezra nodded reticently.

"Anyway, he told me everything is fine. Right?" Her eyes grilled him.

Ezra nodded.

"Yes?" she persisted.

"Yes."

There was a pause. "*Oy*. Anyway. Did you wash *neigel vasser* yet?"

Ezra stirred. "No, I haven't." He walked toward the bathroom.

"*Nu*, Ezra, you know you're not supposed to do anything before washing."

"I just woke up, Ima," Ezra responded in playful annoyance, well within tradition of the close mother-son relationship.

"I brought you your tallis and tefillin," she called out to him as he washed his hands.

He hadn't even thought about that. He had to admit it – his mother was an incredible woman.

He went to work a little tired, but he would manage. He had

slept right through the night in that chair, even though it had been a little uncomfortable.

Somehow he found the bugs in the program he was working on and dealt with them. He called the hospital every so often, and his mother informed him on one of the calls that Devorah was due to be released by the following morning.

At the end of the day he asked Kevin if he knew of a flower store in the vicinity, and with a little bounce in his step and a hum in his voice, he picked up a regal bunch of red roses. He presented them to Devorah, and her face beamed, while Ima looked on proudly.

It wasn't Dr. Michaels who came to examine Devorah before her release. It was the second of the two physicians who had discussed her case on admission. He stepped into the room and quietly introduced himself as Dr. Barry Alexander. He was a little older and a little more cordial. Ezra instantly felt more at ease with him.

"How are you feeling?" he asked Devorah.

"Okay, I guess," Devorah replied, smiling.

He nodded and reached for her chart.

"You're listed here as taking antibiotics. May I ask what for?"

Devorah explained about the sores in her mouth, but added that the pain had almost gone.

"May I take a look at that?"

He shined a little flashlight in her mouth. Then he studied her IV port. The area around it was blue and swollen.

"Did you have an injury in this area prior to being admitted?"

Devorah shook her head.

He noticed another bruise a few inches below, closer to her wrist.

"What happened here?"

"I...I don't know. I must have bumped my arm there a couple of days ago on the railing of a staircase, but it didn't hurt."

The doctor was silent. Ezra stared at the doctor and then at Devorah.

"If it's all right with you," the doctor said, "I would prefer not to release Mrs. Gelb just yet. I'd like to conduct some further tests. Now there is no immediate cause for alarm. I just want to make sure that all the appropriate blood work is completed before her release."

Ezra swallowed. He knew he could press the doctor on what he meant by "no immediate cause for alarm," but he didn't know if it would be wise. Especially in front of Devorah.

"Ezra, the *Tehillim*, please," Devorah requested firmly as soon as the doctor had left.

Suddenly sapped of energy, this small task of reaching for the *Tehillim* on the side table and handing it over seemed to take everything he had.

Devorah launched into the verses. She pronounced each word succinctly and with tremendous conviction. She did not look up for a very long while.

Ezra sank into his chair. Ima had left as soon as Ezra had come in order to prepare a hot meal at home. He debated whether or not to call her. She was bound to start worrying and calling.

The nurses came in to take some blood and left. Dr. Alexander came in again to inform them that the blood work would receive top priority, and there was a strong likelihood that the results would be in by the end of the day.

They thanked him. Ezra called his office to inform the secretary that he would not be in at all that day. Eventually Devorah trailed off to sleep, her book of *Tehillim* flopping onto her chin, rising and falling as she slept.

Ezra tried to read a book Ima had left behind. But every time he completed a paragraph, he felt compelled to look up, to check on Devorah, to glance at the wall clock above the door.

They were both awake when Dr. Alexander entered the room. He pulled up a chair next to Ezra. His face was ashen and his mouth set in a grim line.

Both Ezra and Devorah shut their eyes momentarily.

"I'm very sorry to inform you," he said haltingly, addressing both of them. "Mrs. Gelb has leukemia."

The world caved in.

5

Planting

"Then the king declared, 'Whoever finds my lost treasure will be richly rewarded!' and with a stamp of his royal seal, the king's proclamation was issued throughout the land. Soon the whole..."

"Why is he lying down?" Danny asked curiously, seizing the page and preventing it from being turned.

"Well, in those days the nobility – the very important people – would lean on their chairs. Hey, do we do that, too?"

"Yeah," Danny replied, smiling as he rubbed his palm back and forth over the glossy picture.

"When do we do that? Do we do that all the time?" his *tatty* prodded him, putting his arm around Danny's waist and squeezing him gently for the answer.

"No! Only on Pesach!" Danny asserted, as if to rebuke his father for not knowing the basics of Judaism.

His *tatty* placed a kiss on his forehead and dipped back into the gripping tale of lost treasure, a surreal wonderland that served as a forum for teaching a very important mitzvah.

"And with a proud smile, Avi handed over the last pile of treasure to the king.

" 'Avi,' the king addressed him cheerfully, 'not only have you done my kingdom a great service by returning my lost treasure, but you have also fulfilled the great mitzvah of *hashavas aveidah*, returning a lost object.' "

The story finished, Danny's father recited the Shema with him and pulled the covers up to just below his face. Danny was tired, but his eyes were still fully alert.

"Tatty," he called softly as his father was about to switch off the light and exit the room.

"Yes, Danny."

"Did you see the monster?"

"The monster?"

"There's a monster outside in the field."

His father sat down again on the edge of the bed.

"Danny, don't worry. There are no monsters." He put his hand on Danny's shoulder and kneaded it gently. "If you ever get scared, just come to me, all right?"

The light clicked off, and Danny was immediately besieged by a thick darkness that lost no time in splitting into different forms and shapes, swelling and retracting, floating effortlessly around the room. It was a secret cavorting ground for all those images churned out of his prolific mental drawing board. Life was breathed into them, their forms igniting and sputtering, their eyes raging with steel-blue venom. And then, suddenly, they all made way for something else as a great big breach opened in the far wall. Bricks were thrown everywhere, and the monster, growling and scraping, shoved its way into his room, swallowing up his toys and his chair, stretching out a metal claw to grab at his bed...

His mother flew across the hall to his room at the sound of his petrified scream. She found him writhing in his bed.

"Danny, Danny..." She held him. "It's okay. You had a nightmare. Everything is all right."

She rocked him gently as he whimpered in her arms, unable to get the image of the monster out of his mind.

※ ※ ※

Grandridge had a knack for concocting all sorts of interesting weather at a moment's notice. In the morning, the sun had streamed lazily through calm, unfettered skies. The birds had waltzed languidly from tree to tree, and the browntail moths had flickered dreamily from petal to petal. Now, as Rachel prepared to take Yosef to the doctor for a checkup and to shop for food, she looked up in astonishment to see rain pummeling the bedroom window and a howling wind racing through the trees.

She rushed Danny into the car and buckled Yosef into his seat, then dove into her own seat and discovered that she had gotten almost completely drenched during the minute she had been exposed to the rain.

The bakery was on the way to the doctor's office. She needed some bread and thought she'd also pick up a few bagels for lunch.

They pushed their way through the bakery door and stopped to soak in the dry warmth of this cozy, toasty haven.

"Well, hello there!" the baker exclaimed, popping out of the back room. He was looking at Danny.

Danny smiled shyly.

"Say hello," his mother urged.

Danny emitted a barely audible whisper in response, then turned his attention to a rainbow-colored assortment of cookies that begged to be scrutinized and devoured. He pressed his hands against the glass and gazed at them while his mother placed her order.

"Now you go home and get out of this nasty weather," the baker advised as he handed Danny's mother her parcel.

"Oh, I wish I could," she remarked, snapping open her purse to retrieve her checkbook. "I have to take the baby to the doctor now."

The baker thought for a minute. "Why don't you leave Danny here with me while you go to the doctor? Things are slow today anyway."

She looked up at him. "Are you serious?" she asked incredulously. Things were certainly different in a small town.

"Sure. I could do with a little company when the customers are staying at home."

She continued to gawk at him while her brain processed the possibility of accepting this offer.

"You're so kind," she said finally. "But that's okay. I can manage."

"All right. It's up to you."

She smiled and turned to leave, but stopped short when she faced the exit. It wasn't just raining. It was snowing.

"Oh, my gosh," she gasped. "Is it really necessary to have all four seasons in one day?"

"Welcome to Grandridge," the baker said cheerfully.

She retraced her steps and placed the car seat on the counter.

"Are you sure you don't mind? It would make things a lot easier."

"I'd be delighted. Question is if Danny wants to stay."

Rachel stooped to Danny's height and whispered in his ear. He agreed without hesitation.

🌿 🌿 🌿

Danny watched the bakery door creak closed, making the glass shudder in its wake. His eyes darted to the baker's and waited. The baker immediately invited him to choose a cookie from the offerings displayed. Charged with this very vital mission, Danny set to work at once, inspecting, evaluating, and critiquing. After a very close contest, he eventually singled one out. Within seconds the winner found its way into cookie never-never land.

The baker pulled up a chair for Danny and then began to tell a story. He made up the story as he went, the words rolling off his tongue like paper from a printing press. It had something to do with the snow, the wind, moving to a new town...

Danny was riveted. He held his breath, letting it out only at the end of a string of words punched out by the baker. Naturally the story had a happy ending, and the relief on Danny's face was palpable.

A customer walked in and placed a large order. Danny watched the baker from his chair, swinging his legs as he followed the man's movements around the store. After a while, the baker returned to his seat next to Danny.

"Did you see the monster in the field?" Danny inquired as the baker folded his legs, humming a tune.

"The monster?"

Danny nodded.

The baker leaned forward. "Was it big?" he asked soberly.

Danny's eyes widened. "Yes. Real big."

"Did it have scary eyes?"

Danny thought hard for a moment. "I didn't see its eyes," he said excitedly, sliding off the chair. "But it was so big and running fast, and its hands were big, and it was eating everything up, and I started running away." He was breathing rapidly, his wildly gesticulating hands slowly coming to a stop.

The baker grimaced, his short gray moustache crinkling under his nose. "You must have been very scared."

"Yeah." Danny didn't want to dwell too much on this detail. "I think it still comes after me when I'm sleeping. It doesn't go away."

"Hmm," the baker murmured, narrowing his eyes and stroking his chin. "What are we going to do about this monster?"

"I don't know." Danny shrugged, open to whatever plan of action the baker might conceive.

"Did the monster hurt you when you were running from it, Danny?"

"No. But it was about to."

"Mm-hmmm," the baker responded matter-of-factly, strategically extracting information like a detective. "But the monster never did hurt you, did it?"

Danny shook his head.

"Well, then we ought to consider the possibility that the monster is actually...a nice guy."

"No." Danny laughed disdainfully.

"Really, Danny. Sometimes that can be true."

"But, Mr. Baker, he was so big and...scary."

"That doesn't matter."

Danny sat down again to ponder this novel idea. Information was being sorted and reassembled in his brain.

"How about another cookie?" the baker suggested after a while.

The offer was instantly accepted.

By the next morning the snow and rain had cleared. The sun was out again, and the birds and butterflies were going about their business as if nothing had happened. Danny's mother was rushing to get his lunch ready for school and get Yosef dressed at the same time. Danny was waiting outside by the car, pushing a single pebble back and forth along the gravel, showering his shoes with dust. One overenthusiastic kick drove the pebble past the car and down the pathway alongside the house. Danny ran to retrieve it and balanced himself against the chain-like fence before kicking it back again. He stopped when he realized he was only a few feet away from where he had fallen weeks before. He had not returned to that spot ever since.

His heart racing, Danny pressed his face up against the fence and stared at the field. The ground was still all chopped up and ruined, but there was no sign of the monster. He clutched the fence firmly, breathing in the air of the field. He longed to be there again.

🌿 🌿 🌿

Shimmy Levin defied convention a few days later at school when he became the first kid in Danny's class to come up to him at lunchtime and strike up a conversation. One subject led to another, and soon the alluring topic of an empty wilderness in Danny's very own backyard became the central focus of their discussion.

"You mean there's nothing on it?"

"Yep," Danny replied, blocking the dark image of the monster from sticking its foot through the door.

"And it's right next to your house?" Shimmy sputtered, bits of peanut butter and jelly slipping from the sluice gates of his oral chewing machine.

"Yep," Danny said proudly, taking credit for the field as if he had personally manufactured it.

"Wow!" Shimmy was fascinated. "So can I come over to see it?"

"Sure."

Danny's mother was delighted that he had a playmate. At least it would make a significant dent in her heap of guilt. So she went on a bit of a promotional binge and set out plates of chocolate-chip cookies, chocolate brownies, those unavoidable wafers (which she detested, but Danny loved), slices of fresh watermelon, and two kinds of ice-cold soda.

This would have sufficed to inspire Shimmy to return, but it was the sight of the field, spread out majestically in front of him, that really took the cake. He stood transfixed behind the chain-link fence as Danny excitedly described his expedition in the field that day, leaving out a few details that might frighten Shimmy off.

"Let's go over," Shimmy suggested, his face flushing red and his eyes ablaze.

Danny tried to force the word *no* from his mouth, especially since his cast had only recently been removed. But the word was stifled by his immense desire to do what Shimmy was suggesting. Without formally endorsing Shimmy's suggestion with an "okay," he started climbing the fence and Shimmy followed suit.

Danny's feet touched the ground, and without looking back he began treading the soil. Shimmy joined him, and they both studied the contours of the earth as they walked. Danny was saddened by the damage done by the monster, but he dared not say anything about it to Shimmy.

"What's this?" Shimmy inquired, suddenly bending to the ground and folding something green between his fingers.

Danny inspected it closely. "It looks like grass or a flower or something."

"Wait!" Shimmy exclaimed. "Look! There are millions of them all over."

Danny raised his eyes and saw that rows of these tiny green things extended as far as his eye could see.

"Something's growing here," Shimmy remarked, standing on his toes and lifting his chin so that he could see beyond his normal parameter of vision. "It's real neat."

Danny had to agree. The faint streaks of green that had sprouted everywhere meant that something potentially thrilling was stirring. Perhaps a dense forest with a whole intertwined mesh of hidden pathways and corridors would grow here and beckon to him from across the fence. Or maybe a lush jungle of giant leaves would sprout up that would link up to offer roller-coaster foliage rides. The opportunities for exploration and adventure were mind-boggling.

Danny smiled. For a moment, the destruction of his playing field was just a little more bearable.

6

Ima was trying to force her eyes open as she sat hunched in the hospital chair, but her eyelids kept closing on her like hydraulic doors. She hadn't slept for thirty-six hours. In her mind, to sleep at this point would be shamefully insensitive. She had to do everything in her power to be there for her daughter-in-law, who in turn kept insisting that she go home and get some rest. Every so often this discussion would repeat itself until it reached a crescendo of obstinate selflessness and then fizzle out again to a gloomy silence.

Ezra lay sprawled on the vacant bed next to Devorah, sound asleep after having cried with her for hours into the night. Devorah herself would probably have been sleeping, too, if it weren't for the numerous tests to which she had been subjected. Continual blood pressure checks, temperature readings, saline bag replacements, and various procedures ensured there was never a genuine lull in activity.

Abba came in to announce that the coffee machine was out of coffee.

"Did you try the one on the fourteenth floor?" Ima asked.

"The fourteenth floor? I'll need a cup of coffee just to have the energy to get there!"

Ima flapped her hand. "Forget it. I can do without more caffeine in my veins. Shirley says caffeine is what causes her to be irritable and grumpy all the time."

Before Abba could really outshine himself with an amazing flash of witticism, two people cautiously slipped into the room and stood nervously at the foot of Devorah's bed.

"Mom. Dad," Devorah whispered, her lips trembling.

"Debbie!" her mother cried, immediately bursting into tears. She rushed forward and bent to embrace her daughter, the first time she had done so in years. Slender, elegantly jeweled, fingernail-painted hands stroked Devorah's face.

"Honey, we tried to come on the first flight available, but they were all full."

"Not a seat," her father added from the foot of the bed.

"We waited at the airport for twenty-four hours before there was something available, but it was a connecting flight. And there was a delay. It was just terrible."

"Well, the important thing is you're here," Devorah said.

Her mother turned to face the others in the room. The in-laws greeted each other cordially. She noticed Ezra on the adjacent bed. "Oh, he's sleeping, poor thing," she said, shaking her head.

"How are you feeling?" Devorah's father asked, gripping the bed rail.

"Fine," Devorah found herself saying.

In a strange way it was true. Besides the pain in her mouth, she did not hurt anywhere, and the baby was fine. "I mean, for someone who has…"

There was a long pause. Everyone looked down.

"This disease."

"*Oy*, I'm sorry," Ima said to Devorah's mother, rising to vacate her chair. "You probably want to sit here and talk, and I've been selfishly sitting here the whole time."

"No, no, no. Please don't get up, Lily," Devorah's mother protested. "We really can't stay for very long anyway because our luggage is still in the back of the cab, and he's waiting for us outside to take us home. We literally came straight here from the airport."

"That's okay," Devorah said without a second thought.

Her mother hugged her again, shutting her eyes and planting a kiss on her forehead. "We'll be back later," she whispered, gesturing to her husband that it was time to go. He smiled awkwardly, and they exited the room.

A strange silence hung in the air, like the aftermath of a storm. Devorah's face was turned the other way as she stared blankly at the window. Ima fidgeted with the hem of her blouse, pretending to have just noticed that a few threads were coming loose. Abba explored a number of sophisticated-looking touch-button commands on the wall next to the door. And Ezra began to stir. He sat up in a disoriented haze, fortunate to have missed the whole thing.

Dr. Alexander entered the room just as Devorah was served her lunch meal. Ezra stood up to face him. Nerves jumped at the realization that some form of judgment was about to be passed.

"Well, we have scheduled a cesarean section for tomorrow morning at eleven. As soon as it is possible after delivery we will transfer Mrs. Gelb to Oncology. I have been working closely with them to determine the best course of action." He gave a polite, nervous smile.

Ezra stared at the doctor, searching his eyes. "Thank you," he mumbled finally.

The doctor lingered for a few moments, trying to communicate his sympathy with a concerned smile. He turned to leave.

"Dr. Alexander?" Devorah called.

"Yes, Mrs. Gelb."

"Can I...can I go out for the afternoon?"

The doctor froze for a moment, his eyes darting back and forth like harried squirrels. "Well," he croaked, "I, er, don't see why not. There is more blood work that needs to be done, but that will be done only once you are transferred to Oncology. The baby is not in any distress. Just, er..." He cleared his throat. "Just make sure you don't do anything stressful. If there is any problem, come back immediately."

Devorah smiled at her small triumph. Ezra looked at her like she was a teenager returning after her curfew.

"I want to go to the park," she declared, folding her sheets over as if she were about to jump into the car, IV and all. "I want to see the lake. And I want to see the flowers."

The doctor summoned a nurse to unhook the IV.

The sand path that snaked through the vast bed of lush grass had gotten a little muddy from the previous night's sudden downpour. But now the glistening surfaces of the park were being toasted by a fierce bout of midday heat in another display of erratic weather that made Grandridge famous. The lake lay ahead, at the end of the path. It deflected the sun's ruthless rays with a magnificent crest of shimmering crystal on top of the deep sapphire bowl of water.

They strolled along the path in silence, stopping every now and then to take in the sights. Devorah had thought this excursion would lift her spirits. Instead it appeared to be taking her deeper into a darkening abyss. As she walked along, it seemed that nature itself was closing in on her. How could she pretend? This was not real anymore. She gradually came to a halt.

Ezra turned to her, gazing into her eyes.

"Oh, Ezra!" She raised her hand to her mouth to stem a sudden storm of emotion. "I don't want to die." A jarring cry shuddered through her. "I don't want to die."

Ezra shut his eyes. With these words, she had crystallized both their thoughts into reality. It was too much for him. They both sank to the grass on the side of the path and wept uncontrollably, surrendering to the crushing pain.

The gentle breeze that fanned them while they lay on the grass suddenly gained momentum. Ezra glanced up at the sky through bleary eyes. Only moments before there had been nothing in the sky except a pristine, endless blue. Now clouds in varying shades of gray were swallowing up all the empty spaces, taking position for another spontaneous downpour.

"We should go," he said to her, hoisting himself up.

She rose slowly to her feet, but dropped down again suddenly.

"What's the matter?" he asked quickly.

She breathed through the pain until it subsided. "Ezra, I..." She squinted at him through the remaining sunlight. "I'm not sure, but I think we'd better get there as fast as we can."

Ezra gulped. "I have my cell phone," he stammered, fishing it out of his back pocket. His fingers floated hurriedly over the numbers, but he did not press any of them.

"Should I call 911?" He stared up at her, at a loss.

"No, not 911...well, maybe..."

The wind was getting colder, injected by an icy sting. He could not take any more time for further deliberation and dialed the three-digit number. The woman who answered asked him to describe his location. He gave her the details, and the dispatcher informed him that an ambulance was on its way and that it would contact him shortly. Ezra thought they should make their way back to the parking lot so it would be easier for the paramedics to find them.

Devorah got up again, this time without pain, and they began moving slowly up the path. She stopped abruptly and took a deep breath. "Oooh," she moaned, closing her eyes.

By the time they reached the parking lot, the clouds had merged to completely blanket the sky in a deep woolen gray. The temperature seemed to be nose-diving. They climbed into the car, and Ezra switched on the heat.

"I'm tempted to just drive you there. It's only thirty minutes."

"I know, but we should do this the safe way in my condition."

The windshield began to mist over, then was dabbed by thin white streaks.

"It's snowing," Ezra announced in an edgy monotone. He turned on the radio and scrambled for a weather forecast.

"...snow over the western boundaries. Warm waters combining with a burst of Arctic air will effect a dump of between eight and ten inches in some parts..."

Ezra did not hear the rest of the report, because just then Devorah moaned. "Ezra..."

That was all Ezra needed to hear. He shoved the car in gear and sped out of the parking lot.

"Slow down please, Ezra. The roads will be slippery."

"I want to get there before the real storm hits us."

They were silent for a long while as Ezra swerved determinedly in and out of traffic. The snow had begun to cover the sidewalks and treetops. Fortunately the roads were still mostly clear. A light in front of him turned yellow just as he was at that ambiguous distance away from it. He slammed his foot on the brakes, remembering to pump them in weather such as this. He came to a stop safely within the lines. But he realized Devorah was right – he had to take it slowly.

Ezra turned to his wife. Her eyes were closed. He wiped the sweat off his forehead and tapped his fingers nervously on the steering wheel as he waited for the light to change.

The hospital came into view through the hand-wiped arch on the windshield. He pulled into the emergency entrance, left the car running, and dashed into the reception area. His cell phone rang as he was frantically trying to describe the situation to the nurse. He answered it as soon as he had finished. It was the EMT. He was looking for them at the park. Ezra explained the situation and hung up. As he clicked off, it rang again. It was Ima.

"Ima!" Ezra shouted through his own heavy breathing, the howling weather, and the frenzied response by hospital personnel. "Help! Devorah's in labor!"

Devorah waved to him with a comical smile as she was whisked past him on a stretcher. Ezra could only laugh at the sight. He was breathing a little easier now, knowing they were in the hospital and out of the storm. He glanced back at the street through the entrance. The snow was whipping across the streets and buildings. Now the question was, would Ima make it?

He remembered that he had left his car running. He dashed outside into the blur of white.

When he returned, he shook off the snow and hurried down the corridor, scanning the bright signboards for directions to the delivery ward. He figured it would be close to the prenatal ward, but he wanted to be sure.

He slipped through elevator doors that were just about to close and stood anxiously in the center of the elevator. To his chagrin, the elevator headed down. He hadn't even bothered to check the direction of the flashing arrow above the elevator frame.

Ezra took a deep breath and shifted from foot to foot as the elevator descended lazily to the various levels of the parking garage. Finally, after his fellow passengers exited and after new company entered, the elevator began to make its way upward.

"Devorah Gelb?" he sputtered at the nurses' desk when he reached the right floor.

"Fourteen," a nurse answered immediately, pointing in the general direction of the room.

He stumbled into room 14 and was met by a buzz of activity. The curtain was drawn, and a number of people kept popping in and out through the opening in the curtain. He wanted to stop one of them to ask what was happening, but they were wholly absorbed in their tasks. Then a doctor emerged and marched up to him, pulling him aside. It was none other than that sterling example of chivalry, Dr. Jeremy Michaels.

"Mr. Gelb," he said, clutching Ezra's arm. "Your wife's blood pressure has plummeted. Ideally we would perform an emergency C-section, but it's too late for that. Don't worry. We have everything under control." He patted Ezra's arm and with a smile marched back through the curtains.

Ezra slumped against the back wall, dumbfounded. He noticed Devorah's purse hanging from the side table. He grabbed it and fumbled for her *Tehillim*. If there was one thing he was sure of, it was that everything was not under Dr. Michaels's control. He strained to chant the flowing black letters that pulsated with real power and majesty, drawing his soul into the eternal cradle of strength and grandeur.

He recited the words loud enough for Devorah to hear. He did not care whether or not it caused a disturbance. A nurse appeared from behind the curtain and gave him a thumbs up. Obviously Devorah was encouraged by it.

A nurse wheeled in what looked like a tray, and the activity seemed to step up a notch. Ezra's heart pounded, his trembling hand gripping the *Tehillim* tighter. Suddenly there was a shout for oxygen. He heard it loud and clear amid the clamor.

Just then Ima burst into the room, still caked in melting snowflakes. She ran past all the passing staff members, flew behind the curtains, and before anyone could blink had grabbed hold of Devorah's hand and was whispering into her ear.

Within seconds, Ezra heard a flurry of sharp of movements and orders, and then…a tiny cry, a cry from a human being he had never known before.

"It's a girl!" a nurse shouted.

"*Mazel tov! Mazel tov!*" Ima cried, kissing Devorah's forehead over and over, Devorah, tears streaming down her cheeks, smiled back.

After only a few moments, the baby was presented to her mother, who mustered the strength to cradle her in her arms. "She's so beautiful," Devorah managed to whisper through her tears, her oxygen mask muffling her words.

"Blood pressure is stabilizing," another nurse called out.

"Can the father see the daughter?" Ezra inquired tentatively from the other side of the curtain.

A nurse picked up the baby gently and brought her to Ezra. When he peered into her tiny face, indescribable warmth flushed through him. He held her fingers, or, more accurately, she held his finger, and for the moment all the pain and anguish was just a little more bearable.

7

Harvesting

The overpowering aroma of peanut butter and jelly was the signal to Danny that Shimmy was near. Danny was happily shooting little pebbles through cracks in the branch of the oak tree behind the main office, when Shimmy, sporting a healthy supply of his favorite sandwich, came up to him with a proposal.

"Danny, you know how, like, there's hidden treasure in a faraway land, like the stories my father reads to me?"

"Yeah," Danny replied disinterestedly.

"Well, I have an idea. Maybe in that field next to your house there's hidden treasure somewhere, and nobody knows where it is. If we look for it, we could become like the heroes."

"What's heroes?"

"I think it's a tzaddik."

"Oh."

The sea of peanut butter and jelly in Shimmy's mouth swirled around roughly as he awaited Danny's response.

"So do you want to come over again?" Danny said nonchalantly.

Shimmy nodded eagerly.

Shimmy returned home with Danny the following day. During school, Shimmy had not ceased to remind Danny of the grandness of their impending mission. Danny wasn't convinced that they would find this treasure, but he acquiesced, riding on Shimmy's unfaltering enthusiasm.

After sampling little pieces of each vegetable that Danny's mother had prepared for them (her guilty conscience had now expanded to the area of nutritional substance in the food she served), Shimmy and Danny darted out the back door of the kitchen to the yard.

For Danny, setting his foot in the yard each time was like rounding the dry mountainous terrain that led to Clayton Beach. There, the vast expanse of deep blue sea would unfold before his eyes as each inch of the mountain receded from view. Here, too, the great sizzling stretch of open land presented itself to him as he rounded each corner of the house.

Shimmy ushered him to the fence and proceeded to outline his carefully calculated plan of exploration to Danny, who wasn't able to discern any logic in Shimmy's words.

"How are we going to dig for the treasure?" Danny inquired at the end of the presentation.

Shimmy's eyes darted back and forth. This was a technicality he had overlooked. "Do you have a shovel?" he asked after some deliberation.

"I have a shovel in my closet that I used to take to the beach."

"Great."

Moments later Danny returned with a shiny yellow plastic shovel.

"Wow! That's a great shovel!"

"Yeah."

Shimmy swallowed as he surveyed the field one last time before leading the expedition. He took a deep breath and turned to Danny. "It's time," he announced gravely.

Slowly they began to mount the fence. It wobbled just as it always did, but this time Danny was armed with a shovel, making it even more challenging.

"Give the shovel to me. I can take it," Shimmy volunteered, freeing a hand and extending it toward Danny. Danny passed him the shovel.

"This is a very important thing," Shimmy said, trying to spur Danny on. "Come on, let's get over this fence."

"Boys! What do you think you're doing?" a familiar voice yelled from behind them, instantly foiling a carefully crafted excursion into the hinterland.

At the shock of being discovered, Shimmy fell from his perch on top of the fence and landed on his back. Fortunately his fall was cushioned by his thick coat, which he had tossed aside moments before embarking on his mission.

Danny quickly climbed down and stood waiting to face the

sentence handed down from his mother. As a punishment, they were to remain indoors for the rest of the afternoon. In addition, since Danny should have known better after his previous experience in the field, he would not be permitted to play in the yard for the rest of the week.

This put a damper on the remainder of Shimmy's visit. Danny tried to interest him in his train set, which had only a couple of pieces missing, but Shimmy had lost heart. In any case, he reasoned, he could play with his own train set at his own house. What did he need to come to this new kid's house for if all it meant was playing with some old train set?

After Shimmy left, Danny pushed the toy back into his closet and padded over to his window. From this vantage point, he could see a large portion of the field. It was covered by a carpet of yellow and green grass. This was as close to the field as he would be allowed to get this week.

He pressed his face against the windowpane. The knowledge that it was there, but that it was now completely off bounds, made him long for it even more. He had to do something about it. He was not interested in any treasure like Shimmy was. All he wanted was to feel the earth under his feet and between his fingers and slide through these new intriguing blades of grass that had sprouted and to invent new scenarios of thrilling adventure with the field as his stage.

He stood by the window, transfixed, until an idea popped into his head.

Danny heard the front door slam shut, and his eyes bolted open as they did every morning when his *tatty* left for shul. His father had begun davening very early so he could learn a little before work. Danny would awaken briefly and then fall back to sleep.

But this morning Danny did not turn over and go back to sleep. His eyes remained wide open, staring blankly into the darkness. He turned toward the window and saw faint, colorful streaks of light spreading across the sky. It was unnervingly quiet. Every slight shift of his foot under the bedsheets tore through the silence.

He rose slowly from his bed. If he could get dressed quickly enough, he would be able to dash into the yard, jump the fence, play in the field, and return to his room before his mother woke up.

He took out a shirt from his closet. He had only recently learned the trick of holding his shirt face down before pulling it over his head so that it would settle on him the right way around. But doing this now would take too much time, so he pulled it over him any which way.

After he had gotten dressed, he tiptoed out of his room and down the stairs, holding on tightly to the banister. He reached the back door of the kitchen and, his heart leaping, turned the knob.

It was locked! His eyes traveled up the door to the latch, well beyond his reach. He snuck over to the breakfast nook and grabbed hold of a chair. As he dragged it, it produced a shrill squeak. Danny froze. Upstairs, something moved. He waited for a few excruciating moments, holding his breath. There were no further movements.

Lifting the chair slightly as he pulled it, he brought it close to the door, climbed on top of it, and...*click*. He pulled open the door.

The air outside was crisp and calm. The sky had become velvet blue. He stepped into the yard, treading on the delicate dewdrops that coated the ground.

Still tiptoeing, Danny reached the fence. He glanced back at the house to make sure nothing had stirred, then, facing the field again, he lifted himself up and cleared the fence like a champion. Practice certainly made a difference.

He immediately began to sprint through the grass, soaking in the cool air as it beat against his face and fanned his hair.

Today he was running from the Egyptians, and the great Yam Suf was up ahead. He reached it together with all of *Bnei Yisrael*. Danny beheld the awesome sight. The stalks of grass that were waving and weaving together in the breeze were transformed into the gushing waters of a daunting body of water. How were they going to get across?

And then the sea parted, walls of water piling up on each side. He raised his hand and signaled to the hordes of people to walk on the dry seabed, the towers of water on each side roaring as they passed through.

They reached the other side, an arbitrary marking point of unexceptional stalks. Then he sang another favorite from Uncle Moishy, urging everyone to celebrate with him in song.

The sun had risen and was casting light sporadically over the landscape. Danny took a little break from his pioneering journey through the wilderness to observe how his shadow stretched exponentially and how it could so quickly shrink, depending on how he moved or jumped or lay.

A shadow appeared close to his head. Was that his arm? He moved his arm, but the shadow did not move. He carefully followed the direction of the shadow to its source. And his heart filled with terror.

The monster. He strained against the light to discern the form. It had grown. He stumbled backward. The house was so far behind him. Would he be able to make it back before the monster got to him?

He thought he heard a voice coming from the monster. It shouted something at him, but it was drowned in its own thunderous snarl. He did not wait to find out what it was trying to tell him. He turned on his heels and ran, careening through the wheat stalks toward the house. He tripped on an embedded stone and rolled over, smearing his clothing with mud. He looked up. The monster was still after him but hadn't gained much ground. Still, he wasn't going to take any chances.

Finally he reached the fence and clambered over it. Before dashing into the house, he took one last look behind him. The monster was eating the grass. It was chopping it up and swallowing it. His heart sank. He ran through the back door, pausing to remind himself to close the door gently.

Once inside, he took a deep breath and looked down at his clothing. Mud was everywhere. He quietly removed his sneakers and tiptoed through the kitchen. He heard a thud and spun around. Was the monster at the back door? There was a second thud, but he realized it wasn't coming from the back door. It was coming from upstairs. His mother was up.

His heart racing, he moved slowly along the hall, his muddied sneakers in his hand. Then he heard the creaking of the staircase. She was coming downstairs. He darted into the dining room and hid behind the door. She was heading for the kitchen. Without a moment to lose, he scurried as soundlessly as he could along the hall, up the staircase, and into his room. He shucked his clothes and stuffed them into the very bottom of his laundry pile. He scrambled into his pajamas and dove into his bed, tucking himself under his covers. The very next moment the door opened, and his mother peered into the room, a puzzled look on her face.

"Danny, are you okay?"

He nodded vehemently, still catching his breath.

"I heard you moving around in here. Were you out of your bed?"

"Um...I went to the bathroom."

"The bathroom?" His mother repeated incredulously, listening to his rapid breathing.

Danny nodded again.

"Okay...," she said, a deep frown etched in her forehead.

The door closed, and Danny shut his eyes. But then his eyes burst open again as the image of the monster assaulted his senses. How had it grown like that?

He would not even look through the window of his bedroom. He gazed purposefully up at the ceiling.

Why did it have to eat his beautiful field? It didn't make any sense. First it had torn up his playing field, digging and scratching lines all across it. And then, when stalks of grass had sprouted, offering him a myriad of opportunities for excitement and adventure, it proceeded to rip them up, chewing them to shreds. Did this monster not care at all?

No one believed him that there even was a monster – no one except Mr. Baker. Danny made up his mind to inform Mr. Baker of the latest developments – how the monster had grown and chewed up the grass.

In the midst of his planning the meeting with Mr. Baker, his eyes glazed over and he nodded off, his body sinking into an exhausted sleep only twelve minutes before his mother was due to wake him.

8

In a rare moment, the board members of the Ohr Yisrael shul were unanimous in their decision to hold a *Tehillim* rally for the merit of Devorah Leah bas Rivka. Without much discussion at all, they agreed on the date, the time, and the place. Ezra had not been present, but when he heard of this almost miraculous development, he laughed out loud, but could not hide the tears that were now constantly poised in the corners of his eyes.

They all stood in the social hall, Ezra, Ima, Abba, and Benny and his wife, not to mention the delightful new addition to the family, Sarah Malka Gelb, curled in Abba's arms and sucking blissfully away at her bottle of formula. For years Devorah had dreamed of nursing her baby, the two of them huddled together on the rocking chair, lapping up each other's company while Devorah listened to her favorite Rabbi Avigdor Miller tapes. But that was not meant to be.

The baby would normally have been in Ima's arms, except that Ima was right in the middle of directing, producing, and executing the event that was to commence in the next seven minutes. Although officially she had not been the one to conceive of the idea, nor the one chosen to organize the event, it was part of her makeup to slip her shoulders through the harnesses of whatever was happening around her and bear the yoke. And everyone there seemed to appreciate her doing so; things seemed to flow much smoother when she was in charge.

"The mike has to be under that spotlight, or you won't see the speaker properly," she told a volunteer technician.

"That would be nice, Mrs. Gelb, but the cord doesn't reach that far."

"Get an extension," she replied without blinking.

"Yes, ma'am." He laughed and raised his hand in mock salute.

The next minute she was standing by the entrance quizzing the nice young volunteer who would be handing out the program schedules.

People began filing through the door, and Ima was worried there wouldn't be enough chairs. She turned to a board member. "We need a hundred more chairs."

"A hundred?" he croaked. "Mrs. Gelb, I am not a chair manufacturer."

"There are chairs stacked in the storeroom, aren't there?"

"Yes, but..."

She wasted no time in handpicking twenty young men, some of whom were attendees who had just entered the room. "You can each carry five chairs. You are all young and strong, *bli ayin hara*." They didn't even consider disobeying.

The *rav* of the shul was a gentle elderly man whose boundless love for the Jewish people, particularly for his eccentric little flock here in Grandridge, held him back from retirement. He stood behind the mike, his glasses reflecting the blinding glare of the spotlight.

"We are all here this evening," he began slowly, raising his eyes to address the two hundred and fifty people staring back at him — probably three-quarters of the town's observant Jewish population — "because we care. Look around and see for yourselves how much the Gelb family means to the community, to the people of Grandridge."

Ima fumbled in her purse for her wide-rimmed eighties-style sunglasses.

"We are all deeply shocked and saddened by the plight of Devorah, whom all of you know as a wonderful, devoted..." His voice broke, and he paused a minute to regain his composure.

The *rav* was not the only one in the room whose composure was faltering.

After a while, he continued. "Devorah worked — works — in the shul office. Besides her dependability, her diligence, and her concern for the work she is involved in, there's another element to her character that is a rare find. It is this that makes Devorah Leah bas Rivka stand out from the women of *klal Yisrael*. It is her ability to teach through her speech and, even more so, through the way she behaves how to have *bitachon*, to have trust in Hashem, how to say almost instinctively that this, too, is for the good."

A shuffling of feet and shifting of positions was taking place to the left of Ezra. He turned to determine the cause. Devorah's parents had just arrived, clambering over half a row of people to get to a couple of seats near the front. As they settled into their chairs, his mother-in-law mouthed to Ezra, "So much traffic!" She let out a beleaguered sigh and began to fan herself with her folded program.

"Ironically," the *rav* continued, "we are moving now from feeling mere appreciation for this incredible attribute to actually living through that which she has taught us. We are now faced with a formidable challenge, coping with the crisis our beloved Devorah is now experiencing and saying, 'This, too, is for the good.' "

By now there were a number of moist eyes and quivering lips in the audience.

"As you all know, Devorah has always maintained as her staff and daily staple the eternal words of David HaMelech. She and her *Tehillim* are inseparable. It is only fitting, then, that we gather, as we have done, to draw from that deep well of comfort, to connect to the One Who creates and conducts the world, to recite *tehillim* for Devorah Leah bas Rivka with all our strength, for a *refuah sheleimah*, a complete and speedy recovery."

Everyone rose immediately and began to pour their hearts into each verse as they repeated after the *rav*. The deafening roar was an exquisite melody, a symphony of heartrending cries imploring in unison for the gates of supreme compassion to be opened.

Little Sarah Malka was sleeping quietly in Abba's arms, serenely oblivious to the sparks of sublime energy floating around her. Only when the last beseeching prayer was uttered did she stir and deliver the unspeakable. Abba jumped up in somewhat of a fluster. He looked at Ima and pointed to the diaper. Ima, even through her dark glasses, was able to communicate her message loud and clear merely by staring back at him unsympathetically.

"But the last diaper I changed was Ezra's," he protested in a loud whisper. "And that was cloth, before they invented these modern plastic contraptions."

"Disposables are easier, Abe," she responded dryly.

"That's if you've used them before," he argued. He would have liked to have substantiated his point using the example of driving, that everyone always said it was easy, but until you had actually driven a few times, it was not so easy at all. But he was not afforded this luxury, since Sarah Malka had begun to voice her own high-pitched protests, and it would disturb the proceedings. So Abba had no choice but to forge his way wide-eyed to the men's room.

A small crowd of people huddled around the Gelbs afterward. Ezra tried to thank each of them personally for their presence. It took something like this to gain insight into the power of caring and the power of community. He was charged with an invigorating warmth, one that could only result from the wondrous hidden light of human souls linked together for a lofty purpose. Nothing else on earth could ever match it, no matter its silicone wizardry or exorbitant price tag.

Ima had to excuse herself so she could get back to the hospital. She wanted to run to the store on the way and pick up a jar of mayonnaise for the potato salad she had prepared before the rally.

The visitor's chair next to Devorah's bed had become her second home. It was her bed, her living room, even her kitchen. She had managed to wangle a small refrigerator into the room using her invincible charm. Whenever the hospital food was not quite up to standard (not an uncommon occurrence), she would dip into her hoard of salami, salad dishes, or kugels and offer them to Devorah, although Devorah did not have much of an appetite.

Wading through the extended hands of the remaining well-wishers, Ezra came upon a familiar face. Kevin was standing apprehensively behind the others, his hands crossed in front of him, an uninitiated white satin *kippah* perched on his head.

"I...wish Mrs. Gelb well," he said hesitantly.

Ezra was so touched he gave Kevin a hug. Kevin had outdone himself at work, pleading Ezra's case to the higher-ups and obtaining a favorable response. Ezra would officially be permitted to take as much time as he needed to care for his wife and newborn daughter. Although the term "absolutely necessary" had been used in the agreement, it seemed that this had also been given ample room for interpretation.

Abba returned wide-eyed with Sarah Malka and handed her over to Ezra while he talked to Kevin. "These diapers are much easier," he exclaimed, genuinely amazed.

"You should know —" Kevin swallowed "— I think about that Shabbos a lot."

Ezra smiled.

"I, er, don't use the phone anymore from sunset to sunset."

Ezra gawked, his hand blindly trying to guide the baby's bottle into her mouth.

Kevin seemed embarrassed by his revelation, to him an infinitesimal achievement, but that was not at all how Ezra saw it. He was eager to relate to him the *midrash* about opening one's heart the size of a needle hole and Hashem expanding the hole to gigantic proportions. Kevin had made the first move — a cosmic move — clearing a path for limitless spiritual growth. But before he could voice these thoughts, Ezra was pulled away by a board member who needed to speak with him about the shul newsletter. He made a mental note to resume the conversation with Kevin. He was thrilled by how things had changed and by how HaKadosh Baruch Hu masterfully set things up. This was undoubtedly a night to remember.

🌿 🌿 🌿

Ezra had gotten used to the overpowering smell of disinfectant that pervaded the hospital walls and corridors. The large steel-walled elevators, the passing nurses, the patients and visitors were as familiar to him as the traffic on his daily commute to work. What intimidated him, though, was the chart. A small harmless-looking square sheet of graph paper that hung on the wall outside Devorah's room, it always drew his attention before he entered. He would study it with angst, holding his breath for the moment or two it took to evaluate it. *Please, let the white blood cells go down* was the prevailing hope.

On this particular occasion, there was indeed a dip, but it was marginal, not enough to conclude that she was responding to the chemotherapy. With a sigh, Ezra put a smile on his face and stepped quietly into the room.

Devorah was asleep. Ima's seat was empty, although the hot tea on the table next to it told him it had been vacated only recently. She must have taken the baby somewhere.

Ezra sat down and peered at Devorah's face. She was breathing softly, her face pressed into the pillow. He wondered what she was dreaming.

He sat back in his chair and stretched his legs, staring out the window at the gently waving treetops and the silent stream of cars and trucks on the freeway in the distance. How could life continue as normal out there? How could the sun continue to shine, the wind continue to blow, the birds continue to chirp, as if nothing had happened?

Ima walked in, bouncing Sarah Malka gently in her arms. She mimed a "hello" to Ezra and settled slowly into her chair, passing her granddaughter over to him.

Ezra cooed at his child. She had already begun to smile. They (whoever "they" were) said babies generally started to smile at around five weeks.

"You're right on track, Sarah Malky. You're a big girl, aren't you?" he whispered, stroking his daughter's cheek.

Devorah began to stir as the sun set, leaving behind a striking orange and yellow haze. Ima had fallen asleep, her head leaning against the side of the chair.

"Hi," Devorah whispered feebly.

Ezra smiled. "How are you feeling?"

"*Baruch Hashem*," she replied.

Ezra ought to have learned by now that you aren't going get a negative response from Devorah if she could help it.

He scooted past Ima and brought the baby up to the front of the bed. He held her close to Devorah's face.

"Someone wants to say hello," he said.

"Hi" was all she said, raising her hand limply in a wave.

Ezra was silent, and she averted her face to avoid his gaze. He held the baby a little closer, as if to push the sale, but Devorah turned her face away, gazing up at the ceiling and pulling the blanket closer to her. He saw that her hands were trembling.

"Are you cold?"

She shook her head.

There was a long silence before Ezra withdrew the baby, who had begun to fuss anyway. She needed to be taken home, bathed, and put to sleep.

He rocked her in his arms as he moved quietly toward the door.

"E...Ezra," Devorah stammered.

He turned to face her.

"Please don't be mad at me." Her eyes suddenly swam with tears.

"Mad at you?" he exclaimed, although he had to admit he had felt a trace of disappointment. It vanished when he saw her tears.

"I can't be her mother and not be her mother," she gasped, squeezing her eyes shut.

"I'm sorry," he said, hanging his head in shame. Sometimes he could just kick himself.

"That's okay."

He stared at her from the other side of the room. It was situations like this that only served to increase his respect for her, which in turn inflamed the raw pain inside him until he could bear it no longer. He had resolved not to cry in front of her anymore, so he was left to sit alone, in his car, in his room, wherever he could find a solitary spot. There were times he felt like pulling his hair out, and it was then that he would turn to his friend Aryeh, a person who had always opened his door to him, who listened and imparted advice in a firm yet compassionate way.

Elisheva, Aryeh's wife, set a plate of her chocolate chip cookies in the center of the table. Ezra stared blankly into his glass of seltzer, watching the bubbles pop and merge with each other. He was at a loss for words. What words could he possibly use to describe what he was feeling?

"Ezra," Aryeh said, leaning forward and catching Ezra's eye through the other side of the glass, "where do you think Hashem is right now?"

Ezra looked up at him. "What kind of question is that?" he snapped, his forehead locking in a frown.

"Answer my question," Aryeh demanded, not flinching.

Ezra gave an annoyed sigh. "You want me to say He's with me, with me in my pain."

"Yes, in fact, I do want you to say that. But I want to know something else. Do you feel it?"

A long, heavy silence followed. The air around Ezra was suffocating, saturated with anguish, anger, and tension. He loosened his tie.

"No," he admitted softly. "I feel darkness around me. I feel Hashem has distanced himself from me. I feel He is angry with me. I feel...alone." He fiddled with the glass, turning it around in his hands.

" 'Just like a man afflicts his son, Hashem your God afflicts you,' " Aryeh quoted. "You know that *pasuk*, right?"

Ezra nodded. "It's in *Devarim*."

Aryeh watched him play with the glass. "Do you realize what that means, Ezra? A father doesn't distance himself from his son when he afflicts him. It's precisely because he loves his son that he afflicts him."

"Why is my Father afflicting me?" Ezra still would not look up.

"Now you are asking that age-old question: Why do bad things happen to good people? We all ask that question sometime."

"Yes, and I can answer it from an intellectual standpoint. I can tell people that we have no idea what God's master plan is. We don't see how it all comes together. But now I'm stuck in the middle of it. I don't have the strength to say it. How many times have I sat around this table, trying to internalize the fact that everything happens for the good, that there is a reason Hashem did not give us children for so long? And then, finally, Hashem blessed us with a beautiful baby girl. And at the same time He gave us...this. I have to believe it's all for the good. I know I do." Ezra finally raised his head and focused hollow eyes on Aryeh. "Why can't I do it?"

Aryeh sighed and took a sip of his own seltzer. "You have to know something about yourself, Ezra. You are a part of a very select group of people."

Ezra winced. He did not like to be patronized. It usually smacked of the nerve-grating promotional tactics of a telemarketer.

Aryeh clutched Ezra's arm to hold his attention. "Most people don't get beyond asking why bad things happen to good people. You, however, are asking how to internalize the fact that they do happen for a reason. It means you have accepted that everything happens for a reason. You're just struggling to make this belief a part of you."

This apparently struck a cord. Ezra's frown softened.

Seeing he was getting somewhere, Aryeh continued. "The very fact that you are asking this question means you are deeply concerned about doing the right thing, and you want to remove all the obstacles you feel have been placed in your path. The question you are asking is exactly what Hashem wants you to ask."

Ezra shifted in his chair. He reached for a cookie.

Aryeh leaned back in his chair. When Ezra took a cookie, it was a telltale sign that there had been some sort of breakthrough, that there was something more than just the cookie to chew on. Ezra would typically slip into silence, only punching out the rhythmic crunch of the cookie.

"Mrs. Zimmerman," he would call out eventually, holding his thumb up in approval.

"Does Devorah need platelets?" Aryeh asked in a much softer tone.

"Yes, yes, all the time." Ezra turned to him. "Thank you for offering. We need all the help we can get."

※ ※ ※

From a distance, Ezra could see that the graph paper had been updated. His eyes zeroed in on the chart as he paved a clear path through the passing nurses to get to it.

His face reddened. The line had shot upward. He turned away, dazed. He peeped in from the corridor. Ima was sitting there chatting to Devorah. He could not recall Ima ever having looked at the charts. Up until now he had attributed this to her unfamiliarity with the technical side of things. But now he began to wonder if this was not perhaps a deliberate decision — it was easy to get too hung up on the charts and become an emotional slave to its daily swings. It was all very well when the white blood cell count decreased, but when it rose, how would she be able to sit there like that and chat with Devorah, take care of her and Sarah Malka?

He would not have been surprised if this had been her intention. His mother's wealth of wisdom was skillfully disguised by her pretense of naïveté. Throughout her life this had been her weapon. He remembered the time an air-conditioning company tried to charge her almost double the price they had originally quoted, claiming they had not expected the wall they drilled through to be so thick, she being just a little old lady who didn't know from "notin' an' all." So she obliged and toddled off to get her checkbook. When she returned, she commented how fortunate she had been that these wonderful air-conditioning people had come to her rescue.

"I am so grateful you told me about the wall," she twittered, testing the flick button of her pen. "Now at least everyone will know about it."

The burly, jagged-toothed workman stared at her in surprise. "Wait! What do you mean, everyone will know about it, ma'am?"

"Oh," she said sweetly, flapping her hand, preparing to commit her pen to paper, "my husband is the editor of the *State Consumer Magazine*, and I am going to tell him to warn everyone out there to check if their walls are too thick before they install their air conditioning. He'll mention that your company so kindly pointed it out to us after you installed it." She let out a sugar-sweet laugh. "I'm sure you won't mind the publicity — two hundred thousand readers, you know. So how much was the total? I tend to lose track of things in my silly old state."

Ezra happened to be on the phone with Abba at the time, and Abba had related the whole thing from where he sat in the bedroom. Both he and Abba had chuckled under their breath at the prospect of someone attempting to swindle Ima. They both knew it was just not going to happen.

There was a tap on his shoulder, snatching him away from his pleasant reverie, dropping him at the chart, the hospital room, and...Dr. Jeremy Michaels. Great.

"Mr. Gelb, It's a good thing I caught you. I don't have such great news."

Ezra was used to his style (or lack thereof) by now. The man may have had a medical degree, but he most likely flunked the bedside manners credit.

"I've just checked in with Dr. Harding, and he wants to talk with you."

"If my wife is under his care, then why were *you* looking for me? This is Oncology."

"I know where I am. As I said, I just checked in with him." The doctor raised his face muscles in a smile. "He told me if I see you, he needs to speak with you." He gave Ezra that detestable little slap on the shoulder and marched on, his flaky hair lifting like an airfoil.

Dr. Harding was thankfully much more approachable. He had a sallow tint to his skin and seemed to be eternally tired. Perhaps it was because he was so busy, or perhaps it was because he bore the burden of so many suffering patients.

It was difficult to find him. He had an office somewhere but was rarely in it, flitting from ward to ward, patient to patient, his coat flapping regally behind him as he flew.

Finally Ezra spotted him exiting a room at the end of the corridor. He was in the midst of instructing a nurse, who listened attentively and nodded at the end of every point. Dr. Harding spotted him out of the corner of his eye as he finished.

"Mr. Gelb, let's go sit down in the waiting room."

The journey to the waiting room took an eternity, a very silent cruise down the corridors.

Ezra sat down, wringing his hands.

"Mr. Gelb. As you know, we have been giving your wife chemotherapy. Unfortunately she has not responded to the treatment as effectively as we would have liked. Now..." He noticed the pain in Ezra's face, and his own face tightened in sympathy.

"Now what would be ideal is to introduce a second round of chemotherapy at a much higher dosage. The problem with this is that it will weaken her extensively. There is a reasonable chance, though, that she will pull through."

Ezra put his head in his hands. His fingers trembled, struggling to hold his head.

"I guess we don't have much choice," he whispered finally, shutting his eyes.

He was too weak to stand. After the doctor left, he lay down, stretching his legs across two or three chairs. He thought of their precious little daughter, blissfully unaware of the tragedy surrounding her, hardly knowing who her mother was. Would he be able to bring her up all on his...*no!*

He jumped to his feet. He would not let such thoughts enter his head. Why was he being such a wimp? Hashem wanted him to act on this, not sit and drown in a pool of sorrow. There were so many tools at his disposal.

Ezra strode determinedly out of the waiting room, down the corridor, and into his wife's room. He smiled at Devorah and Ima, who were discussing the ideal thickness of a cheesecake. Without saying a word, he fished inside the drawer for the *Tehillim* and carried it out of the room. The various models of cheesecake that were under discussion crumbled in an instant. The women knew something was up.

He sneaked into a small supply room, closed the door, and pushed aside a couple of broom handles. He opened the *Tehillim* and infused all his strength, all his tears, all his breath into the words. He rocked back and forth on his toes, the veins in his neck pulsating as he enunciated each word. He realized at that moment how often he did not pray with the proper intent. Now his mind was solidly focused as if nothing else existed in the world. If only he could carry that energy over to all of his other, seemingly mundane communications with his Creator. The bitter truth was that had all this not happened he probably would never have davened like this in his entire life. Was this happening to him to force him to daven properly?

He knew that there was an idea like this in *Chazal*. But then again, like Aryeh said, who knew why this was happening? Right now he knew what he needed to do: to pierce the heavens with his weaponry of words, to activate an earthly petition with the paper that God Himself had provided. A massive operation was now being officially launched, no holds barred, from the poky confines of a hospital supply room.

※ ※ ※

"Friends," Ezra began from behind the podium. The *rav* had been more than happy to let Ezra address the congregation on Shabbos morning after the Torah reading. It saved him from having to unearth a *drashah* he had given thirty-seven years previously, and he had a suspicion there were some congregants old enough to remember it.

"Although I do not wish any of you to be in my shoes, or in the shoes of my mother, my father, and…my wife…" He read word for word from his notes, which quivered in his hands. He was usually not afraid of public speaking. But when the subject took on momentous proportions, something he believed could rock foundations and tear up decrees, he trembled more out of awe than fright.

"I nevertheless wish that you could just step in and step out very quickly so that you all can get an idea of what it feels like to be the recipients of so much kindness, so much concern, so much compassion from our community.

"Many of you have volunteered to donate platelets, a fairly lengthy process. Many of you have offered to take care of Sarah Malka. Many of you have offered to take care of us, we who stand vigil by Devorah's bedside almost around the clock.

"There are also many of you who plead with me, 'What else can I do for you?' It's almost like I would be doing you a favor by letting you help us out.

"Well, I don't know who would be doing who a favor, but I do have a request. We have all heard something about the power of Torah study. We know it changes worlds, breaks barriers, transcends time. This knowledge accompanies us through our lives, through our every day. But how often does it strike a deep chord in us, enough to inspire us to transform that knowledge into something practical and concrete? Instead of discussing the infinite potential that Torah study promises, how often have we made a conscious decision to make it real?

"There are many things this trying time has taught me. I am probably not even aware of all the things I have learned. One thing that stands out, though, is, I have to make it real.

"I know it seems unfair and even selfish for me to expect you all to climb on the same bandwagon, but I would like us all to make it real. I would like to propose that after the *kiddush* each Shabbos we break up into learning partners or groups and study for a half-hour in the social hall."

There was not even a murmur of dissent in the crowd. What would normally have elicited an objection, a groan, or at least a sigh this time caused only an enraptured silence.

"May this new program be in the merit of Devorah Leah bas Rivka, for a full recovery."

A loud amen resounded through the shul.

It seemed everyone was rushing through the *kiddush*, eager to begin this new program. Instead of the congregants chatting away, liver pâté and crackers resting nobly on fingertips, there was much less small talk and the excitement was palpable.

Ezra asked a few people to help him carry some desks, chairs, and, of course, *sefarim* to the hall.

The *rav* sat down with a Gemara at one of the tables and was immediately joined by five or six people. A number of men partnered with each other to learn Mishnah or Gemara. On the women's side, Mrs. Cantor, a teacher at the school, invited several women to her table to learn *Rashi* on the week's Torah portion. Ezra took a second to behold the sight before he joined the *rav*'s table. His eyes sparkled and his spirit soared. The beautiful noise of the *Tehillim* rally continued from where it had left off. Surely something was stirring now in the Upper Realms.

The elusive bug was taunting Ezra. Whenever he thought he'd tracked it down, it would slink slyly from under his grasp, disappearing through the digital cracks of cyberspace. He had to have this program ready, bug-free, by the end of the working day. When would he ever be assigned the task of creating a program rather than fixing everyone else's foul-ups?

"Ah!" He spotted it. How many times had he scrolled past that piece of coding?

"Ah! Eh!" Sarah Malka echoed. She had been lying quietly in her infant seat, kicking her legs. The office staff had been extremely tolerant of the gurgling, screeching, and whining emanating from the general vicinity of Ezra's desk, not to mention the far from subtle aroma that graced the air every so often. It seemed to brighten their day to have a little ball of unspoiled innocence in the office.

This would never have gone down in his old job. Ed would probably have turned psychotic.

He glanced at his watch. It was time to go. He slipped on his coat and covered Sarah Malka with her blanket. Hillary from the front desk flashed past and dropped an envelope on his desk.

"What's this? A bonus?" he quipped.

"Who knows?" She laughed. "I stopped reading everyone's mail after I got sent to prison." She hurried off to get to some other employees before they left for the day.

He scanned the envelope. It was from the company's medical insurance. Did he really want to read this now? He decided against it. He placed the envelope on his "to do" pile and suppressed any panic-stirring thoughts. He was going to see Devorah now, and he needed to walk in with a smile on his face.

※ ※ ※

Devorah beat him to it. A smile lined her face even before he entered the room. Instead of inspiring Ezra, it saddened him. He knew her smile was a combination of disorientation and concealment of pain. She was pale and gaunt, her body a delicate shield against the merciless medical invasion that had besieged her. Much of the time there was nothing she could do but give in to the surreal, drug-induced perception of what was going on around her, where the yellow-saddled tricycle of her childhood was just as real and tangible as the IV bag being replaced by her side.

Often he or Ima would strain to hear an idea or thought she was trying to express, only to shrink back when they realized it was a totally incoherent statement. This was especially difficult for Ima. It was hard for her to witness a mental decline in a woman close to half her age, especially someone she regarded as the daughter she never had. She would get up from her chair on the pretext that she was refilling the water container in the bathroom and wouldn't emerge for a long time.

The chart always beckoned. Ezra couldn't help it. Though he always debated with himself as the chart blipped onto his radar screen, it would always get the better of him. *The eye sees and the heart desires*, he would remind himself. *Try not to look at it.* But it was difficult.

His heart skipped a beat. Today the white cell count was down. It wasn't just down; it was really down. He burst into the room. "Ima! Did you see the chart?" he blurted, knowing full well that she never looked at it.

Ima stared up at him expectantly.

"It's really down!" he exclaimed, rubbing his hands together. "Did Dr. Harding come in today?"

"No, not yet. He said yesterday he would be in at about six-thirty this evening. What's the time now?" She grappled with her wristwatch to get a reading.

"It's 6:45!" Ezra declared. "He's late!"

"You sound like my wife," Dr. Harding said, smiling, as he entered the room. It was obvious his smile was not just triggered by this little interaction. His face was radiant.

Ezra held his breath.

"I am happy to tell you that this round of chemotherapy has had a profound effect on the cancerous cells. We are not entirely in the clear yet, but we are almost there."

Ezra closed his eyes and breathed a haggard sigh. He and Ima stared at each other in silence. They both turned to look at Devorah, whose eyes were closed. She lay very still, bedecked with tubes and swabs.

"Devorah?" Ezra called softly. There was no answer.

He called her name again, a little louder. Still she did not respond. Ezra withdrew. She was probably in a deep sleep.

🌿 🌿 🌿

That night, his *ma'ariv* was an outpouring of gratefulness. While everyone else in the shul was heading for the coatrack and digging into their pockets for their car keys, Ezra was still in orbit, cherishing this respite, this lifting of some very heavy, paralyzing clouds. He began to have visions of how it would all turn out, the glowing picture of him and his wife released back into the world of normality, playing with their daughter, worrying only about work deadlines, peak-hour traffic, and the price of diapers. This picture was not just a wishful puff of colorful images. It was a real possibility. He just knew it.

It was a long time before he turned out the lights on this utopian scene playing in front of him.

*   *   *

A distant shrill sound merged with the college examiner's stern rebuff when Ezra walked in late for the exam in his pajamas. The examiner started slowly dissolving into powder, but the shrill sound grew in intensity until it surfaced and shot right through the sleep barrier.

The phone. He bolted out of bed.

"Mr. Gelb?"

"Yeah." His heart was pounding relentlessly against his chest.

"This is Dr. Olkers. We met briefly once before. I have to advise you to come to the hospital as soon as possible. Mrs. Gelb has had kidney failure and is showing signs of lung failure. We…" The doctor sighed. "We don't expect her to make it through the night."

The room began to spin. Ezra dropped the phone.

9

The Mill

The front door closed, a mild click that stunned the fragile silence of the early morning. Danny's eyes snapped open. He immediately felt the bedsheets underneath him. No! It had happened again.

He pulled the blankets closer to him and lay in the dampness. He was trapped. He could not tell anyone of his shameful failure. The only thing he could do was lie in it and wait for it to dry. He wondered if his mother had noticed that his bedsheets were wet lately. What would she think of him? She always told him what a big boy he was, but if she knew, maybe she would say he was like Yosef, just a baby.

He stared up at the ceiling. He would not look out the window at the dim forms and shadows that lay out there. His bedroom was very high up, so he was sure the monster couldn't get through the window, unless it had grown even more since the last time. He turned his face toward the wall, trying to block out the image of the monster. He ran his fingers along the tiny white granules of the paint, back and forth, waiting for his mother to come and wake him.

🪶 🪶 🪶

"All right. It's time for recess," Rabbi Silver announced. The rest of his words were drowned out by the raging stampede of eager arms and legs blazing a trail through the chairs and tables to the playground. It was pointless to put any restraint on this free-flowing surge of bottled-up adrenaline. Rabbi Silver completed his sentence as a mere formality. "Please be sure to come straight back to class as soon as the bell rings." He knew he was the sole audience for his words, not unlike the stewardess's request that everyone remain seated until the aircraft came to a complete stop.

In any case, he had behaved exactly the same way as a child. And some of these rambunctious little tigers would grow to be upstanding rebbes and teachers, who in turn would ponder how to deal with the next generation of human energy tanks. It was an interesting process.

After the door slammed shut, he stretched and yawned and returned to his desk. He had some preparation to do. At this time of day, though, he dreamed of a soft bed in a dark, well-heated room. If it weren't for the fact that he had misplaced his watch the night before, sometime between helping with the washing up and tucking in the kids, he would not have had to squint to read the wall clock at the back of the classroom. And if it weren't for his reading of the wall clock, he wouldn't have noticed Danny still sitting there at his table, rolling a crayon between his fingers.

If a kid stayed behind during recess, it meant one of two things. Either something was clogging the adrenaline jet stream, or there was a leak in the adrenaline supply. But a kid generally did not make a conscious decision to enjoy his break indoors. Only adults would ever consider doing nothing an attractive form of entertainment.

He approached the boy and sat down in a chair across from him.

"How's it going, Danny?"

"Fine," Danny said, his eyes centered on his revolving crayon.

"Do you like it here?" Rabbi Silver asked. With a kid you could skip the small talk.

Danny didn't answer, which was an answer in itself. It was obvious that he was still struggling to integrate into the school. The rabbi knew how difficult the kids made it for a newcomer to be accepted. It was a very long process in a small town. But with Danny it seemed to be taking longer than usual. And now, for the first time, the boy was forgoing his recess period.

"Do you still think about the city where you came from?"

Suddenly Danny's eyes filled with tears. He looked up at his teacher. How he wished he could get rid of the field, the monster, the fence, the wet bed, and Shimmy just like that. "I want to go home!" he exclaimed suddenly, bursting into tears. "I want to go home!"

Rabbi Silver picked him up and held him in his arms.

The tower stretched to the sky, or at least to the level of the dining-room table, which for the ant scurrying through the fibrous fringes of the rug, was a daunting skyscraper. Danny tried to cajole the ant into climbing the tower to experience just how majestic it was. But the ant seemed disinterested, perhaps afraid.

"Don't worry, I'm not going to hurt you," Danny assured it, but it seemed to flee every invitation to come closer.

He was left to appreciate the structure on his own. He felt a little guilty for building his own Tower of Bavel, because Rabbi Menkin had said that the people who built it were not very good. But, he told himself, he was sure they did not use old shoes and sandals that had been designated for Goodwill as their building materials. He had wanted to see if it worked, and it did. He lay flat on the floor, his head raised to the top of the tower, admiring his construction from the ant's-eye view.

"Danny," his father called, approaching from the kitchen, where he and Danny's mother had been talking quietly.

Danny's face turned from the skyscraper to his father's towering form. From the way his father was standing there looking at him, it seemed this was not going to be just a quick question. Danny jumped to his feet. Maybe his father just wanted to spend some time with him.

"Can you read me a story, Tatty?" he asked excitedly.

"Danny, come sit with me." His father led him to the couch.

Danny sat on the couch, his hands clasped over his lap. He looked expectantly at his father.

"Danny, Rabbi Silver spoke to Mommy today. He says you're

sad about being here. Are you sad?"

Danny looked down. He kicked his legs rhythmically in the air, his heels gently tapping the couch bottom.

His father gave him a hug and whispered, "Your bedsheets are wet. Do you know that, Danny?"

Danny's face flushed. He tried to get out of his father's embrace. He wanted to run far away, to the other end of the house. Maybe he would even hide in that small scary room underneath the staircase.

"Danny, why don't you tell me what's making you sad?" his father urged, trying to maintain his hold on him.

Danny shrugged. He stared at his feet, which had slowed to a stop.

"I want to go home," he whispered eventually. There was just no other way he could express it.

His mother suddenly appeared in front of them. She had been waiting in the wings, listening in. She crouched to Danny's level, signaling to her husband that she was about to try a new angle.

"Danny, right now we can't go back. But I'll tell you something. Tell us what you would like to do now, something you would enjoy, and Mommy and Tatty would let you do it as a treat, if we can." She glanced at her husband for his stamp of approval.

Danny stared into his mother's eyes. There were endless opportunities, from playing catch with his Tatty outside to a bicycle ride in the empty lot next to the supermarket. But there was one thing he really, really wanted.

"I want to go to Mr. Baker," he declared with a trace of a smile on his face.

His father gave his mother a baffled look.

She, too, was a little perplexed, but she soon understood. "He means the baker." She told her husband about that crazy afternoon when she had taken Yosef to his doctor's appointment.

Danny's father turned to him. "Does he give you cake and cookies?"

Danny nodded.

His father smiled. "You know, I can understand what they say, that the way to a man's heart is through his stomach. But I never thought it would start so young."

Rachel returned the smile, but only as a matter of politeness. She was not satisfied. Her little boy was sitting right there in front of her, but it seemed as if he was a million miles away. She was pained by the feeling of helplessness this evoked. Although her husband behaved as if this was a minor problem, she knew he was just hiding his distress behind a veil of confidence. It had always been difficult for him to admit to a problem. He was an all-or-nothing type of guy, and if something was wrong, he feared that everything was wrong.

"It's 6:20," she said. "I hope the bakery is still open."

Sure enough, the baker was closing up his store. At the end of every day, he would gather a large portion of the leftover products into large bags and bring them over to a woman in the community who would distribute them to needy families.

When he saw Danny approaching with his mother, a puffy hardened doughnut with a chocolate crust was diverted at the last minute from its destination and directed toward Danny. Danny asked no questions and offered his palm as a parking place for the approaching doughnut.

"Danny would like to spend a few minutes with you," she explained nervously.

"Sure!" the baker agreed without hesitation as he tightened a bag securely with a long twist tie.

Rachel sighed in relief. She hoped this would make her son happy. "Are you sure you don't have to run anywhere now that you're closing?"

"No, not right now. I do have to drop these bags off, but I can do that later, on the way to the *Tehillim* rally. You know about that, right?"

"Yes, for Devorah Gelb. My husband is going." She shuddered, thinking about the trauma the Gelbs were going through. It made her own worries seem infinitesimal. She should be counting her blessings and chided herself for all the foolish things she worried about.

"So until then I would love it if Danny would keep me company," the baker said.

"I'll pick him up in half an hour?"

"Even an hour should be okay."

Danny was still munching on his doughnut when his mother left. This time he was unperturbed by her departure. The door rattled the windows as it closed, but he was too busy making himself at home with his doughnut to notice.

"Did you see the monster again?" the baker inquired casually as he loaded a plateful of cookies into a new bag.

Danny stopped munching. How did he know? He held the doughnut tightly in his hand, long enough for the jelly to start oozing out the sides.

"I have a feeling you did see it," the baker remarked before Danny could muster a response. The boy's expression had been a dead giveaway.

"He grew bigger!" Danny exclaimed, his eyes ablaze.

"Hmm. Do you think he's been eating something?"

"Yes, yes!" Danny wanted to jump up and down, but he was afraid his doughnut would catapult from his hand.

"Well, what do you think he's been eating? Spinach? Spinach makes you grow, you know."

Danny was unsure. "I saw it eating grass. Does grass make you grow?"

The baker paused. Eating grass. Could this be a clue as to what the boy was dreaming about? Perhaps a grass-eating animal he had seen at the zoo?

"I don't know if grass makes you grow. I've never tried it. Yech!" The baker made a face.

Danny giggled, flashing his milk-white teeth.

The baker was inspired to provide an encore of funny faces, ranging from the lazy grass-eating cow to the nimble cross-eyed chipmunk. But the best one was the brawny fat-lipped bulldog.

The baker's twitching gray moustache was perfect for this beastly portrayal, sending Danny into fits of laughter and globs of jelly streaming down his hand. It was the first time Danny had laughed like this in a long time.

"You know, Danny," the baker said, sealing the last bag and sinking into a nearby chair, "we have to do something about this monster."

Danny's face was instantly solemn. The last of the doughnut disappeared down his gullet.

"You want to know a secret about monsters?" the baker whispered, looking over his shoulder. "They are scared of you."

Danny gave him a puzzled look.

"It's true. They try to scare you. They look big and frightening. But the minute you stand up to them and tell them to go away, they get all scared and run away."

Danny was stunned. The stampeding giant mass of crushing metal and gnashing claws that swamped his mind suddenly shrank to a pleading metal beetle overturned on its back.

"Really?" he asked, sitting up straight, his face beaming.

"Uh-huh," the baker nodded assuredly. His eyes narrowed as if to emphasize the magnitude of this highly classified information.

"Can I have a cookie?" Danny asked, shattering the gravity of the moment. His eye had caught a multicolored caramel-vanilla medley still happily ensconced on the shelf.

The baker laughed. He rose to grab the cookie and hand it to his young friend.

"So," the baker continued, trying to reinject some seriousness into the conversation, "what I want you to do, Danny, is something for big boys only. I think only you can do it. Are you ready to hear what it is?"

Danny nodded, smiling. He put down the cookie.

"The next time you see the monster, even if he's grown bigger, I want you to go up to him and tell him loudly to go away."

Danny stared up at the baker, absolutely still.

"Do you think you can do it, Danny?"

The image of the field, the fence, the damaged soil, and the half-eaten grass flooded Danny's mind. Instead of valiantly pushing it all away, he let it stay. Then he pictured himself transported back onto it. He began to tremble, but not out of fear, more out of cautious excitement.

"What do you say, Danny?"

"Okay," the boy said softly. He dwelled on this illustrious mission for only a few moments longer before he was lured by the venerable feast of flour and sugar in front of him.

🌿 🌿 🌿

Bubby Chana had come to Grandridge to babysit for the day. Danny's parents were attending an all-day parenting seminar at the shul given by a visiting rabbi from Eretz Yisrael. This had been another guilt-ridden decision on the part of Danny's mother. How could she leave her son for a whole day? Was that healthy?

Of course, the most logical counter to this concern was that she was, after all, attending a parenting seminar, which could help her to resolve her dilemmas and relieve her guilt pangs in the first place. But allowing logic to supercede emotions was always difficult.

The midday sun penetrated the living room, instantly gilding the furniture and floors in its path. Danny was halfheartedly wheeling his dump truck across the rocky terrain of the floor tiles, looking for a spot to dump his load, which consisted of a giant (relative to the truck) tennis ball and a loose puzzle piece.

"Danny, why don't you go play in the yard?"

Bubby Chana must have noticed his lackadaisical attitude to his game, and it had dawned on her that such a nice day was wasted spent indoors.

He jumped up and ran to the back door, stepping slowly down the patchy clay stairs. He faced the field head on, thinking about Mr. Baker's words. He could see the man's piercing eyes and twitching moustache as if the baker were standing in front of him now, with the field and the great blue sky as his background. Mr. Baker was spurring him on in an urgent whisper, the words merging with the gentle breeze that brushed his skin. He ran up to the fence, then glanced back at the house. Bubby Chana was probably engrossed in her knitting. She was forever at work on junior winter wear. This time Yosef was to be the recipient of thick yellow stretch pants.

It took him a little longer this time to climb the fence. It swayed and buckled under him. He had lost some familiarity with the tricks of the trade.

His feet sank into the ground. The soil was not as choppy as it was before. It seemed smoother and drier. The grass that had escaped the monster had shrunk, drooping to the ground.

Danny raised his eyes and surveyed the scene. It was in ruins, glaringly and painfully void of all signs of life. This is what had happened to his plans of gliding through a lush thicket of teeming plant life. How cruel it was that the monster should be permitted to wreak such havoc under everyone's noses and only he and Mr. Baker were aware of it.

We have to do something about this monster.

Mr. Baker's words rang in his ears loud and clear. He could even feel the mushy texture of that last bite of doughnut against his palm.

He swallowed hard. He was on the monster's home territory.

They are scared of you.

Danny tried to visualize this great jumble of menacing metal as a whimpering goggle-eyed puppy. It had been easier to do in the bakery.

He stepped forward, crunching the dry stalks that lay scattered across the field. He kept his eyes straight ahead, on the lookout for any suspicious sights or sounds. He picked up his pace, striding smoothly across the field. So far there was nothing but the never-ending rows of withered plants that disappeared into the stark boundless blue of the sky.

He began to tire. Kids tended to forget that their bodies were corporeal entities that could run out of gas. Danny continued on anyway, puffing through the field, his feet beginning to drag.

Just when he thought he had to sit down, he saw something ahead of him. But it wasn't coming at him. He stopped, holding his sides and staring at this new creature.

It was a long white building, and alongside it was something else he could not make out. He looked back over his shoulder to check if somehow, through a cruel twist of fortune, Bubby Chana had been following him all this time. But she hadn't. In fact, Danny couldn't even see his house or the fence he had climbed. In fact, he had no idea which direction he had come from. A stinging panic surged through him, that supermarket-aisle-where's-my-mommy panic.

His lips trembling, he decided to push ahead. He had never been this brave or reckless before. He was being swept forward by the powerful words of Mr. Baker. But if his mommy would find out! He cringed. Would he ever be able to find his mommy again?

He came closer and closer to the building and the indiscernible object alongside it. He crouched low, his eyes straining to distinguish its form. He gasped. The monster. But it wasn't moving or making any noises. Maybe it was sleeping. He moved forward, his heart thudding. He had to be very careful. The last thing he wanted to do was wake the monster. It seemed that all of Mr. Baker's assurances eluded him now, at the moment of truth.

Then a strange thing happened. He had gotten close enough to the monster that it completely filled his vision, and he had been observing how its metal glinted in the sun, when he began to think that this monster...was not a monster. He stood straight up and marched over to this...thing. It had enormous black wheels, a shiny yellow frame, a driver's seat, and a steering wheel. It was not unlike one of his toys that were still packed away in the last remaining boxes.

He sighed, disappointed and relieved at the same time. So this was not the monster. It looked very much like it, though. The real monster must be lurking out there and could pounce on him any minute.

He heard a creaking noise. He staggered backward, dropping to the ground. Without a moment to lose, he slithered along the gravel and hid behind one of the big, bulky wheels.

Cautiously, he took a peek from behind the wheel. An old peeling door to the white building had been opened. He waited there, poised behind the wheel. There were no further movements or sounds. The sight of an open door to a building like this was a powerful magnetic draw; it was like a current that seized him and was dragging him in. Emboldened by his progress thus far, Danny crept along the gravel toward the building.

"Ow!" The pebbles hurt. He scrambled to his feet and dashed toward the door, slipping through the entrance.

It was the largest room Danny had ever seen. A zillion of his bedrooms could probably fit inside it. He wasn't sure exactly how much a zillion was, but the way he had heard it used, he was sure it was higher than a hundred.

He moved further inside, his eyes boggling at the height of the ceiling and at all the strange-looking slides that zigzagged all over the room. He strode over to where one slide dipped to his eye level and peered inside. It was filled with chopped parts that looked a lot like the beautiful grass from the field. Then it dawned on him.

This was where the monster had taken its food. This was probably its house.

A chill spread over him. Just as he was about to turn on his heels and race for the door, a deafening boom thundered through the building. Danny screamed, but he could not even hear the sound of his own voice. The slides all across the room were moving, and then a terrifying sight: the contents of the slide were being pulverized into smithereens by a monstrous mesh of machinery.

He sprinted toward the door, not looking back, sobbing through his wild screams. The worst was yet to come. He got to the door, and it was locked shut.

10

The moment never came. The whole night Ezra, Ima, and Abba stood around Devorah's bed, their nerves on edge. Even Devorah's parents were biting their nails from the other end of the room. A profound sadness permeated the quiet night air, stifling any desire for conversation. Moist red eyes gazed at the pale still form in front of them. Nurses floated in and out of the room, switching this and adjusting that. If it weren't for the oppressive mass of machinery inundating her, an observer would have no idea that the patient was on a spiraling decline.

Ezra lifted his eyes from the threadbare *Tehillim* to see the sun pop up over the horizon and begin to sparkle with the first light. That unthinkable moment had still not arrived. He turned to look at his wife. Her breathing was steady and deep. Behind her ravaged exterior was a seasoned fighter. She had always believed in the value of life. And now he saw how such a determined philosophy had seeped into her bones, providing her with a fortress of strength in her battle for life.

One thing was clear to him, and he said it out loud, the first words to crack through the vacuum of sound in the room.

"The doctors are wrong. They said they didn't expect her to make it through the night. But look, the sun has come up."

This prompted everyone to stare out the window at the incandescent ball of fire that illuminated the world. They watched its progress as it launched itself above the mountains, hovering in a majestic orange haze. It was as if they were welcoming a royal dignitary, a harbinger of good news.

It was not long before daylight trickled into the room and the nurses changed shifts.

The pace outside the room became more harried, phones rang, intercoms sounded. Routine rushed in, somehow producing a calming effect on the family. Abba had already dozed off in a chair, Sarah Malka curled up snugly in his lap. Ezra's eyelids struggled courageously to stay open. Ima had sunk into her chair, raising a tenacious eyelid for a moment before it dropped closed.

Dr. Harding entered the room, followed by an entourage of people Ezra did not know. They all came to a halt at Devorah's bed.

"We are astonished," Dr. Harding declared after a quick scan of the charts and machines. His excitement defied his pervasively sallow complexion.

"There has been a significant improvement in Mrs. Gelb's vital signs. Her kidneys are functioning normally. This is highly unusual."

Warmth rushed into Ezra's raw nerve endings. His hands fumbled blindly for the psalms of thanksgiving in the *Tehillim*. He had undoubtedly found himself on a screeching roller-coaster ride. The dips were gut-wrenching and came hard and fast, and the upswings were breathtaking and came just at the lowest possible points. The trick, he mused, was to hold on to the rails and never let go. He gripped his *Tehillim* tightly.

"In addition, our tests have revealed that there is no trace of regenerating cancerous cells. All the new white blood cells are healthy. Of course, you are aware that this by no means indicates she is cured, but if things continue this way for a significant time, we are looking at a remission."

The speed at which the good news hit was strangely enervating. Devorah's mother closed her eyes and clasped her hands together, her bright fingernails pinching her knuckles. Devorah's father stood by his wife, incapable, as always, of expressing himself in any form other than stalwart protector. Abba, who had been startled out of his doze with the doctor's arrival, hugged Sarah Malka closer to his chest. Ezra was overcome and reached for the nearest chair. And Ima, well, Ima was the exception. She was moving about the room, dodging past everyone else, who stood stiffly, like figures frozen under a spell. She was filling the water container, jotting down what she needed to pick up at the store, and already trying to figure out the logistics of caring for Devorah at home.

"Would you like some tea, Doctor?" she inquired as if he was her guest stretched out on an armchair in her living room on a lazy Sunday afternoon.

"Er...no. No, thank you," he stammered, thrown slightly off balance.

"Are, you sure? Because I'm making some now for myself," she continued in her casual vein, picking up Devorah's fluffy slippers and placing them together neatly under the bed. "I have regular and chamomile, although...Abe, you were supposed to remind me to get chamomile. We've almost run out because it's so soothing and relaxing. And it's exactly what we need. Although, come to think of it, we are all so tired right now, it's probably the last thing we need. A good dose of caffeine would probably do the trick, and that we have plenty of. I don't really pay much attention to the experts who say caffeine is bad for you. They're always changing their minds. One minute they'll tell you that it's the best thing for you, and the next they'll tell you it'll kill you with big flashing red letters in your junk mail. You did say you wanted chamomile, right?" Ima looked at the doctor with raised eyebrows.

"Well..." The doctor cleared his throat. "I..."

It had not really been a question. She presented him with a cup of steaming hot tea and cleared a chair for him.

"Drink it. It's good for you. It will put some color back in your face."

Color did come to his face, but that had been before he took a sip of his tea.

"Now," she declared, wiping her hands, "who is the gentleman behind you?"

The small group of attendants began to squirm.

"Ima!" Ezra called from his chair. He stopped her before the whole thing turned into a tea party.

"But they need something hot to drink so early in the morning," she protested. She did retreat, though, and the doctor heaved a sigh of relief.

"That's the service elevator, Abba," Ezra cautioned as he and his father left with Sarah Malka still bundled in his father's arms. Devorah's parents followed at a safe distance.

"Oh," Abba remarked in an exhausted stupor, abruptly swinging himself around to follow his son. The baby waltzed along with him without a murmur.

They all boarded the large, empty, squeaky-clean elevator and stood in silence. Although the elevator was roomy, the forced intimacy between the adults was somewhat claustrophobic. Devorah's father loosened his already loose tie.

Devorah's mother cleared her throat. "Em...why don't you let me the hold the baby?" she addressed Abba. She adjusted her snakeskin purse over a padded silk shoulder and extended her hands in a clear show that her request was more an exercise of her grandparental rights than a helpful suggestion.

"Oh, I'm fine," Abba stated, suddenly wide awake, holding the baby closer.

Devorah's mother dropped her smile, her lips twitching as the elevator cascaded down to the lobby.

Bing!

Ezra breathed a sigh of relief as the doors whooshed open and let out the electric air to disperse into the lobby. They merged with a stream of visitors, patients, and hospital staff, and Ezra hoped that even though they had both parked outside on the street the crowd would separate them.

Devorah's mother could have allowed the crowd to separate them, but now that her sensibilities had been affronted, she had all her battleships lined up and engaged to strike. She slipped ahead of the line and barricaded the front entrance, an automatic door that kept trying to shut on her. Her husband stood meekly by her side, more of a chaperon than a player, although it was clear she was communicating the same thoughts that swam around in his head.

"No one is leaving this building until I get to hold my only grandchild." Her words shot through her lips on a puff of steam, her nostrils flaring. People squeezed by her, giving her an annoyed look. But she didn't care.

"Please," Ezra begged. "You can hold her. Let's just move out of the way." He was not one for making a scene.

"I will move when I'm holding Sarah Masha!"

"Sarah Malka," Abba corrected her calmly.

"Whatever!" she yelled. "You people give them such outlandish names. Why anyone would do that to his child…"

Ezra felt humiliation wash over him, momentarily sapping him of strength. He turned to his father.

"Abba, just let her hold the baby."

Abba handed over the baby, wrapped in her thick woolly blanket, still sleeping. Devorah's mother embraced her grandchild, her face softening somewhat. She stared smugly at Ezra and proceeded to move out of the way of the doors.

"You won't have to worry about me falling asleep with the baby in my arms."

Abba's face turned red. Ezra was stunned. He had often wondered where Devorah had come from. She was the polar opposite of her parents. It dawned on him right there and then that his wife's absolute devotion to the way of the Torah was an outgrowth of the blatantly immature upbringing she had received from her parents. She hardly ever spoke about her childhood, and given Devorah's nature and that of her parents, now he could fully appreciate why.

"It has come to the attention of Leonard and myself," Devorah's mother declared, her eyebrows arched and her nose tilted up, "that my granddaughter may not be receiving adequate care while her mother is confined to bed. Now don't get me wrong. I'm not blaming anyone for anything. I realize we are all living through trying circumstances and it is hard to maintain any semblance of normality and routine."

She aligned her feet together neatly and stood perfectly straight. She relished such moments of unadulterated self-expression, the temporary fulfillment of her theatrical megalomaniacal fantasies that could tear her away from her embarrassingly menial life as a housewife.

"My husband concurs with me that the most appropriate course of action would be to let us take care of the baby while everyone else is indisposed. Lily and Abe are tending to Debbie, and you have to work. A corporate environment is not exactly the best place to raise a baby."

Before Ezra could say anything, she swooped in again.

"And the advantage of our taking care of the baby is that Leonard and I are retired" (as if she had ever been in the workforce) "and we have both the time and the financial means, which, frankly, we all know you don't have."

Ezra wished he could be this woman's father for just a few moments. He would send her immediately to her room without dinner, and the whole thing would blow over by the next morning.

But he wasn't her father, and he had certain obligations to her as her son-in-law. He would have no choice but to weather the insults and the melodrama and try to remain even-tempered. As far as her taking the baby, that did make him a touch uncomfortable. He was concerned that the only reason she wanted the baby was because she had been denied her. It was obviously the principle of it that concerned her most. She had never before expressed any interest in the baby. Was this just a childish "I want that" demand, where the interest in the toy waned after the acquisition was secured?

His thoughts were interrupted by the high-pitched shriek of his cell phone.

"Ima?"

"Ezra! Come quick. I can't...get..."

"What? Ima? What's going on?"

"It's okay. I just can't..."

Ezra could hear her heave and strain. He jammed the phone into his pocket. "Abba, we'd better go!"

"What?" Abe stammered, suddenly panicking.

"I don't know," Ezra breathed as he raced for the elevator. He couldn't believe this. This roller coaster was wearing him paper thin.

He and Abba burst into the room and stood transfixed at the sight that greeted them. Devorah's bed was surrounded by several exasperated nurses, pushing and pulling, shouting commands excitedly. And Ima was entangled somewhere in the middle, swamped by a blur of white. Yet this was not what captivated Ezra and Abba. What caused their jaws to drop was the sight of Devorah standing on the bed. No, not just standing — jumping on the bed, wires flying about her, shouting coherently and accurately the words of David HaMelech.

The words were streaming out of her mouth as though she were in a heated conversation. They were drowned out here and there by the urgent shouts of the nurses, who were struggling to restrain her and pin her to the bed, but the explosive force of her voice was unmistakably real, unmistakably alive.

Tears welled in Ezra's already bloodshot eyes. He could only stand back and watch this spectacle with unstinting admiration. Devorah's underground struggle had finally breached the surface, erupting with such great force, providing all who witnessed it a glimpse into the engine room of an iron-willed fighter. He was so proud of her. There were no words to express it.

Eventually Devorah calmed, lying back down again and slipping instantly into a deep sleep. Ima went about making tea again, her hands shaking, yet managing to hold the filled cups without spilling a drop. "I didn't know she was so fluent in *Tehillim*," she remarked, raising her eyebrows as she sipped her tea.

"I don't think she is that fluent," Ezra said. "I think it was her subconscious mind speaking. I don't know how aware she was of the whole thing."

Ima was fascinated. "I wonder what I have in my subconscious."

"That I'm right most of the time," Abba suggested, not missing a beat.

Both Ezra and Ima nearly dropped their cups as they struggled to contain their laughter.

"Good one, Abba," Ezra congratulated him. Even Ima had to admit, that one ranked pretty high up on the scales.

"Where's Sarah Malka?" she asked suddenly, all signs of levity evaporating.

"Ah, she's, uh...," Ezra stammered. He and Abba stared at each other. Only now did they realize that Devorah's parents had not followed them into the elevator. "She's with...Mom and Dad downstairs in the lobby."

There was a long silence during which a whole wordless conversation took place. Knowing eyes locked with knowing eyes, and a string of unspoken concerns were batted out with each blink of an eyelid.

"So maybe I should go and check on her," Ezra said, and he strode quickly out of the room.

It took a long time for the elevator to arrive. Ezra paced the floor. Was it his imagination, or did everything truly switch to slow motion when he was in a hurry?

As the crammed elevator barreled downward, thankfully not stopping at every floor, his mind began to conjure up a terrible scene. He hoped he was wrong, that his fears would not materialize, that some modicum of decency pulsed within their veins. Surely they would not think of doing the unthinkable. After all, they were certain to have realized the possible legal ramifications of any rash behavior. And that they could be tracked down, if it came to that.

The doors slid open, and his heart sank. They were gone. He could not quell the sudden flames of anger licking at his insides. This was his daughter. He would let them get away with a lot of things, but not this.

He stood there, glaring at the vacated space in the lobby, now trod on by a marching army of shoes. He was rearing to go, but he had no idea how he was going to do this. A little voice was telling him that the confrontation required forethought and prudence. But it was overshadowed by a much stronger, darker voice, the notorious inciter of primitive drives, the master of all sweet illusions of reality. It was telling him to skip the planning. Just go! After all, it argued, you are utterly exhausted, and you cannot be expected to tolerate your daughter being snatched from under your control.

He decided he would compromise. Chazal advise people to be slick when it comes to dealing with the *yetzer hara*. "Confuse it with compromise," as Aryeh would say.

He would get some sleep, not a lot, but enough to restore himself to at least a functioning level. It would not take any of the sizzle off his fury, he assured the *yetzer hara*. He would just delay acting upon it until he had rested a little.

The problem was that when he finally hit his pillow several minutes later, the guilt sank in. It flooded his muddled brain and jolted his nerves. How could he sleep when his daughter had been taken from him? Just as warm, soothing sleep would attempt to close in on him, distant alarm bells would ring and intensify until his eyes were pried open. After thrashing around for a while, he jumped to his feet.

The world was spinning. His heart was racing. He stared at the clock. Almost 11:15 A.M. He did not even want to count how many hours he had been up. He was in no condition to begin this pursuit. But he realized there was no working around something so obviously instinctual and deep-seated as parental angst. It was as if he could reach out and touch this pull, arms flailing, to the immediate pursuit of his daughter.

He jumped into his car and sped off to an address he could vaguely remember.

🌿 🌿 🌿

The driveway was a perfectly chiseled rolling pavement that twisted through a thick carpet of manicured green. The huge grounds were bare, unlike the last time he and Devorah had been there. It was for her father's sixtieth birthday celebration, or perhaps *celebration* was too puny a word to describe it. *Extravaganza* would be more fitting a description of the day's unabashed overindulgences. It wasn't just the seven-man jazz band touting their genius so loudly that conversation could only be conducted as a shouting match. It was also the "floating fruit tray," a band of silver-coated foam boards bulging with exotic fruits, floating in the center of the large, crystal-clear swimming pool.

Ezra cringed at the memory.

Ezra emerged slowly from his car, his eyes scanning the length of the sprawling, boldly shaped clinker-brick home. It had large, wide windows, each one sweeping almost the entire length of the wall it occupied, so that the structure looked more like a glass house sprinkled with just a little bit of brick. Standing in the imposing entrance court, he rapped the golden snout ring (or so it looked like) on the elaborately carved door and waited.

Architects certainly knew how to design buildings so intimidating that they knocked the wind out of their visitors. He felt like a submissive ant. Not to mention the eerie silence that made him feel quite alone against the giant.

He had already sensed that he was, in fact, alone. He stood in the courtyard, trying to delay the onset of this realization, along with its bizarre implications. The last thing he wanted to do was confront the possibility of his in-laws having truly turned into outlaws, the actualization of all those crude dinner-table jokes.

The little cards he always received in the mail with pictures of abducted children popped into his head. He visualized his baby girl ensconced in one little box and his mother-in-law in the other. But he kept staring at the door, hoping it would suddenly open and redeem Devorah's parents from a most deplorable judgment.

Eventually he sat down on the courtyard steps, resting his head against an ornate pillar that smelled of fresh paint. Should he call the police? Should he break down the door? The whole thing was so ludicrous it had all the trappings of a vivid dream. Except that dreams were not so tiring. He could not recall ever having gotten tired or out of breath in a dream.

His eyes closed. It did not take long for the winding walkway ahead of him to merge with the furry bushes, the hanging brass chimes, and the blurry picture of his wife and daughter imprinted on his mind.

🌿 🌿 🌿

"Ezra!" A loud voice startled him out of the doze he'd drifted into.

"What? What?" he stammered, uncurling himself from his contorted sleeping position.

"Ezra, what are you doing on our front steps? What happened?" his mother-in-law cried, dropping her shopping bags and crouching over him so that her pearl necklace hung loosely from her neck.

He jumped to his feet, not caring about the stars whizzing around him.

"Where is Sarah Malka?" he demanded angrily.

"What do you mean, where is Sarah Malka?" she said, wide-eyed. "We don't have her."

Ezra's stomach lurched. "Where's dad?"

"He had to go to a meeting. He'll be back in —"

"What did you do with my daughter?" he raged, his insides turning to fire.

She staggered backward, her ivory-white heels buckling under her.

"I..." She was a tat intimidated. A rare occasion. "Do you mean after I held her at the hospital? I gave her to your father."

"What!"

"Yes, I gave her to your father," she repeated, this time more confidently, realizing that her dignity was about to be restored. It was only a matter of seconds before her smugness would be revived.

"But I was with my father when we realized we had left the baby with you!"

"Yes, but we didn't stay downstairs after we saw you run up there like that. Obviously something was wrong with Debbie. We tried to follow you in the next elevator, but it was full. We actually had to wait a long time for an elevator. Finally we came to Debbie's room. I gave the baby to your father in the hall and checked in on Debbie. You weren't there."

He stared at her, his eyes bulging under the deep furrow of his eyebrows.

"That doesn't make any sense."

Her jaw dropped. "I beg your pardon."

"I said that doesn't make any sense. My father would have called me by now. He knows I'm looking for her."

Her eyes grilled him. She raised her hand slowly to her chest and took a deep breath as if she was about to assume the role of Violetta in *La Traviata*.

"Are you somehow implying, Ezra, that I...that we..." She could not continue. She grabbed her bags and stormed past him to the front door.

Then it occurred to him. He reached inside his pocket and pulled out his cell phone. He had turned it off. He must have unwittingly clicked it off after receiving the call from Ima to come upstairs. He turned it on. Eleven messages.

He scanned through all of them. Ten out of eleven were from Ima. One was from Kevin. His parents were probably baffled by his sudden disappearance.

When Ima answered, Ezra didn't even have to ask if she had Sarah Malka with her. He immediately heard his daughter's contented little gurgles and squeals. Now all that was left was to explain his own seemingly peculiar behavior and to somehow stave off the pangs of humiliation creeping up on him.

When he got back inside the car, he could only sit there, slumped in his seat, his hand on the key but not quite willing to turn it. He couldn't shake the feeling that someone was watching him. Nothing that invoked the proverbial shady, collar-drawn image of the psychotic stalker. Rather, it felt like something supernally devious was deliberately setting traps for him, as if he had been selected to receive a bag of cruel surprises. He would not be surprised if he suddenly heard a voice laughing, cackling with a sinister echo. It made everything seem so dark. What kind of game was this?

🌿 🌿 🌿

"It is like a game. You know that, Ezra," Aryeh said in his gravelly voice.

"Yeah, I hit the nail on the head again, didn't I?" Ezra scoffed, staring at the untouched stack of cookies on the Zimmermans' table.

"That's right, you did. You know life has all the qualities of a game, though a very serious one. And you know that all of these challenges have been deliberately placed in front of you – to test you to see how you deal with them."

"Well, I'm not doing very well, am I?"

"I can't measure how well you're doing. *You* can't even measure how well you're doing. In any case, you can't be expected to master your reactions overnight. It takes time – a lifetime of working on yourself, Ezra. A lifetime."

Ezra sighed, his fingers playing with the rim of the cookie plate. He made the plate swivel like a postcard display stand. He looked up at Aryeh with a frown.

"How does that work?"

"How does what work?"

"Well, we've always talked about how we don't know why things happen to us. Hashem has His master plan, and we, being so limited, can never attempt to understand it."

"Yeah."

"But now you're saying the reason this is happening to me is to test my reactions to it. You see, you're telling me why it's happening."

Aryeh smiled in approval and patted Ezra's arm. Ezra pulled away. He was not interested in scoring points.

"It's not a contradiction," Aryeh explained. "When you accept that everything happens for a reason, a reason you cannot comprehend, then you are reacting to it appropriately. In other words, you still don't understand why these things are happening, and how you react to that very fact is what Hashem wants to see."

Ezra was silent, trying to think it through. The words and concepts eventually slipped into place. It was so simple, really, that he had to laugh.

"What's so funny?" Aryeh inquired, puzzled.

"Nothing," Ezra said, laughing again. "I guess you have a way of getting to me." He made that revealing move for the cookie plate, and Aryeh was able to sigh in relief.

※ ※ ※

Ezra sat at his desk, which was now almost entirely covered with documents, envelopes, and paper files lying in neglected piles, spilling onto each other. No one had said a word to him about his growing workload, about the deadlines he had not met, about the memos he had not read, the meetings he had not attended. They all seemed to understand and to care, a phenomenon so uncharacteristic of the corporate climate. This went far beyond the farce of the daily smile-muscle stretch that so commonly was deemed enough to fill the quota of company compassion.

Ezra had never known a situation where the bottom line actually took a back seat to the human element. In all his working years, he had grown accustomed to friendliness in the business world only when it did not compromise the balance sheets. As soon as that would happen, some creative scheming would ensure that the employee wholeheartedly understood the necessity of his resignation.

As he sat there, combing through every document, he felt a tremendous loyalty to his new company, the kind that inspired selfless dedication to his work. This in itself, he mused, was a masterful corporate strategy.

In a few hours he would be taking Devorah home from the hospital. It would be the first time she would be leaving the ward in over two months. Ima, of course, had launched into a whirlwind of preparations, and an endless supply of food and medications awaited Devorah's arrival. Now he thought he should make at least some headway in all this clutter, to achieve at least something before he had to leave again.

Some mail fell to the floor as he reached for his pen. When he bent to pick it up, bold red letters stared up at him from an item at the bottom of the pile. He picked up the envelope, which dated back a few weeks. He remembered now. This had been sent from the insurance company. He swallowed hard. Why had he put it off? He should have opened it as soon as he had gotten it.

He skipped through the introduction to the relevant paragraph. When he finished reading it, he began to laugh. It was the kind of laugh that was common in the locker room of the losing baseball team as they mocked their own ridiculous performance. This was just too much. Now, ironically, he really could believe that what Aryeh said was right. It was so blatantly obvious that he was on an unpredictable obstacle course that the reality of it earned a great big laugh. He sat back and read the letter again, just to confirm that this was the actualization of another sudden onslaught set to throw him off course.

What was he supposed to do now? He called the number at the bottom of the letter. He went through the usual runaround before he realized he should just press 0 if he wanted to hear a human voice.

"The letter is correct, sir. That's what it shows on file." The woman on the other end was very polite even as she was coldheartedly sealing his doom.

"Is there any way I could get an extension on that deadline?"

"I'm afraid not, sir. Our policy with regard to suspect preexisting conditions requires proof that it was not preexisting to be furnished within the allotted time period. That time period has elapsed."

He may as well have been speaking to a robot.

"Look...what's your name?"

"Kara."

"Kara, I had to switch to your insurance company when I began working here only a few months ago. But I can get people to vouch for me that my wife became ill only after I started working here. They would never have hired me in the first place if they knew my wife was seriously ill and it would affect my work performance."

"I understand, sir. That is why you were given time to provide this information together with a confirmation from your wife's primary caregiver. Since this period has elapsed, there is nothing further we can do."

"But if I was preoccupied with taking care of my wife, was I expected to open my mail?"

"You may write a letter of complaint that will be reviewed by a supervisory panel. Would you like the address for that, sir?"

"No, I...could I speak to your manager?"

"If you give me a number where you can be reached, a supervisor will contact you, sir."

He was obviously not the first person to ask for the manager. He wanted to remind her that the medical costs involved were staggering. It would ruin him financially if he were to become solely responsible. But he realized that there was no point in trying to convince her of anything.

He put the phone down and glanced at his watch. He would have to leave soon. The last thing he wanted was to welcome his wife home with a heavy heart. He had to somehow forget about the money for now. It would not be the most difficult thing to do anyhow. Money seemed so insignificant in the shadow of a life-threatening illness. What mattered was Devorah. What mattered was life and the opportunity to exist in Hashem's world. Life was an earthly link to the Infinite Realm. And money? Money was only a tool from Hashem to be used for good. If He didn't want him to have it, then so be it.

※ ※ ※

The moment Devorah was helped through the entrance of their home, she began to cry. The familiarity of it tore at her. It beckoned her to become a part of it again, but at the same time it reminded her of how far she was from it. In the hospital, it had been clear that her world had changed. Every day she had fallen deeper into her illness, dragging all that surrounded her along with her.

But her home had lagged behind in the time warp. The little

seashells still surrounded the base of her houseplant in the entrance hall. The porcelain honey jar in the glass cabinet had not budged from its corner on the top shelf. The silver candlesticks on the dining-room table glimmered as they always did in the sunlight.

Ima guided her down the hall to the bedroom. Devorah stopped when she caught sight of Sarah Malka's room. Her weeping stopped, too, as she gazed at the teddy bear wallpaper, the white crib, the foam changing pad, and the stuffed toys lining the shelves above it. She stood there for a long while, hanging onto Ima's arm, not uttering a word. No one urged her on either.

In the center of the room was a brand-new wooden rocking chair, as yet uninitiated. Ezra watched her stare at it. He had purchased it the day before. In the store he couldn't decide whether this would be a kind or cruel idea. Now he waited anxiously for her reaction. Finally, she turned.

"Abba," she gestured, holding out her arms limply.

Abba gave her the baby, and she stepped slowly into the room on her own. She lowered herself into the rocking chair and placed a trembling hand across the baby's waist.

She looked up at her family and whispered, "Please close the door."

Ezra fumbled for the door handle and closed the door, leaving the three of them facing each other speechless. Ima headed for the kitchen, slipping on her sunglasses even though she hadn't worn them outside. Abba went to bring in the bags from the car.

Ezra sauntered off to the dining room, where he sat in his

chair and contemplated a pile of mail he had been avoiding. He figured that the hospital bills lay sandwiched in there waiting for him. He picked one out at random, opened it up, and glanced at the figures. He wished he could make in a year what he was being charged for a month. How was he going to do this?

He did not want to approach his parents about this. Not only did he not want to burden them with this additional problem, but he knew that they would just as soon go bankrupt without a second thought to help their son. Of course, there was the option of Devorah's parents, who could probably dole out the money with a flick of a wrist. But he wasn't exactly in their good books of late. There had to be a better way.

The doorbell rang.

Kevin stood nervously in the threshold, his wheat-stalk hair waving slightly in the wind. In his hand he carried a big box of chocolates in a ribbon.

"I checked that it should have a *hesher*."

Ezra smiled. "A *hechsher*."

"Right. It's hard for me to get used to the *hof* sound. Will you still accept it?"

Ezra laughed.

They sat around the table, talking about the company's new branch across the country. The excitement of the expansion had somehow filtered down to the lower-level employees, who really had nothing to do with it. But it made them feel like they were part of something big. Kevin said his father hadn't slept for weeks in anticipation of the move and had spent an inordinate amount of time in the air and in hotels, working on finalizing the plans.

The conversation was not flowing, and Ezra sensed there was something specific on Kevin's mind.

"Kevin, is there something you want to share with me?"

Kevin went red. "How did you find out?"

Ezra shifted in his chair. "I...I didn't. But now you can tell me what you thought I found out."

"I'm engaged," Kevin said, a smile trying to break out.

Ezra's eyes lit up. "A nice Jewish girl?"

Kevin nodded.

Ezra threw his arms around him. "*Mazel tov*! That's great!"

Kevin grinned sheepishly. "You're the first person to know."

"What! Are you serious?"

"Yes. That's why...that's one of the reasons I came. I wanted to let you and your wife know what a profound influence you've had on me. You know I went around with all these ideas in my head of how things should be. I'm sure you picked it up from me when you first met me."

Ezra kept his face impassive.

"Well, just being around you and your family led me to think that, hey, there really is something to this, you know? I realized I had such twisted perceptions of this lifestyle, and ironically it offered something that looked so incredibly deep that I...I know this sounds funny, but I wanted to reach it. Does that make any sense?"

He did not wait for Ezra to answer. "I went on the Internet and discovered this Orthodox rabbi who answers questions, and we've been corresponding by e-mail ever since. I've never actually met him, but he is incredibly inspiring and he takes out time to write me long messages. He can tell that I need it. So that's how...that's why I thought you should be the first to know. You and your family started the ball rolling."

"And this girl?" Ezra croaked, trying to shake off his shock. It felt like he had been awarded the Nobel Prize for a feat he had not accomplished.

"Well, the girl I'm marrying is actually from my high school, but we lost touch when she went off to a kibbutz in Israel. A few months ago I enrolled in a basic Hebrew course in the city, and it turned out she was my teacher."

"You're kidding!"

Kevin shook his head. "You won't believe it, but she wants to keep a kosher home. And she can't wait to meet you, by the way."

Ezra's cheeks reddened. He had never thought of himself as an icon in any form. "You should tell your father" was the only thing he could think of to say.

"I will, don't worry," Kevin said, laughing. "I'll have to wait for him to get back from Singapore. It'll be too hard to track him down there."

Ima passed by on her way to check on Devorah.

"I feel like I want to thank you and your family in some way," Kevin said.

"The chocolates look good to me."

"No, something more than that. I mean, some way I can really help with all your...suffering."

Ezra sighed. It seemed clear that the doors were being opened for him, just waiting for him to step inside. But he hesitated at taking advantage of a friendship. He had never been one to try to benefit from the trust he had built up with a person. On the other hand, here was Kevin extending him the golden scepter. It was his chance.

"Kevin, I know this may sound...I don't know how it may sound." He unfolded a medical bill and presented it to him. "The company insurance won't pay," he declared, throwing his hands in the air. "I was wondering if your father could have some way of—"

"Chutzpah!" Kevin interjected, his face clearly expressing his indignation.

Ezra went pale.

"How could they do this to you?"

"A..a..amazing, isn't it?" Ezra stuttered, breathing a sigh of relief.

"No, you don't understand. This insurance landed a group contract with our company after promising that it would stay away from worming in the preexisting condition stuff in the cases they knew full well were not preexisting. That's why we changed insurance companies. The one we used previously tried every trick in the book to avoid paying." He shifted in his chair, trying to shake his anger.

"I guess that's what it's like out there in the —"

"Well, that's not the way we want it," Kevin asserted, as if he were the CEO himself. "That is not what they promised us."

Ezra had a fleeting sentiment of compassion for Kara, who might lose her job over this. But it really was fleeting.

"I'll tell my father about this," Kevin said, clasping his hands together. "Don't think of it as a big favor. I would say you're doing the company a favor by revealing this bit of information. The only problem is..."

"He's in Singapore."

"Right. And when he comes back, he's off again for meetings about the new branch. I'll probably have to e-mail him about my engagement." He gave a faltering smile, teetering between disappointment and acceptance. This was the father he had known all his life.

"As for me," Kevin added, "I'm still a very small fish. I don't think I have the kind of sway this sort of thing requires."

With this admission, all the air went out of his impassioned defense of the company. He had given himself his own stark reality check.

"You know, very small fish have much more room to move in the bowl," Ezra remarked.

Kevin laughed.

※ ※ ※

The summer sun blazed over Grandridge, the mountains in the background barely visible in the haze, lending the skyline a blue-gray hue. The pallid gray concrete of the distant city was a barely discernable line on the horizon, strikingly silent from this vantage point, like a ghost town. The air was muggy, but in the shade of the lumbering trees of the park, it was tolerable.

An ant somehow managed to leap onto Ezra's arm the moment he leaned back on the picnic blanket with his watermelon. He wondered how they always managed to do that. It took them less than a second to size up their target and latch onto it. Their tenacity was something to learn from. Shlomo HaMelech said that by studying ants you could also learn an aversion to stealing...

"Ezra," Ima said, snatching him from his musings, "would you get Devorah's pills from the car? I forgot them. They're in the glove compartment. Which reminds me, I haven't put my new car insurance thingie in the glove compartment yet. I always forget, although I have never been stopped yet, so it doesn't make much of a difference. Your father, on the other hand, drives so fast that..."

"I don't drive fast," Abba retorted, wiping a bread crumb from his chin.

"So how come we're always getting speeding tickets when you drive?"

"Their instruments are faulty. I think it has to do with a delay in electronic data transmission."

She looked at her husband as if to say, "You can't be serious," and he looked at her as if to say, "You can't be taking me seriously."

Sarah Malka, in the meanwhile, had crawled off with alacrity as soon her little footsies touched the ground, and since it had been only a few seconds since Ima had set her down, no one had imagined she would gain so much ground. Devorah looked up to see her munching merrily on a neighboring family's sandwich while their backs were turned. She grabbed Ima's arm and pointed frantically in that direction. "*Oy!* Ima!" was all she said.

Ezra returned to receive a full report of the incident from his father, whose twinkling eyes revealed a tremendous pride in his mischievous little granddaughter.

Ezra went up to the family to apologize.

"I can replace the sandwich she nibbled on," he offered the woman who had been laughing at a joke her husband had just told. The woman told him he shouldn't worry about it.

The distance back to the picnic blanket was short, but it seemed to stretch forever in his mind. The image of that family and their laughter pained him to the core. His own family was having a picnic as if they were just like everyone else, but they weren't like everyone else. It didn't matter that Devorah had been in remission now for a few months. It was still there, hovering over them wherever they went.

Once, a few years back, he and Devorah had been bumped off a flight, and the airline put them up in an upscale hotel they would never have otherwise been able to afford. Walking around the lobby and riding the elevator, they rubbed shoulders with people who could certainly afford it. Rather than delight in this little feel-good distraction, they had not felt very good at all. They had been all too conscious that they were merely transposed onto the scene, not truly a part of it. This was what he was feeling now as he strode the short distance to the blanket. They would never be truly part of the scene again.

He sat down and poured a drink, still absorbed by these thoughts, although his mood lightened when he saw Devorah smile. She was watching Abba roll from side to side as Sarah Malka tried to grab a clump of his hair. The smile lingered, but she said very little. She had grown much quieter, as if her personality had slowed along with her body. Ezra knew her silence came from a new awareness. She was someone on the brink with an acute appreciation of existence, and life was not to be treated lightly.

※ ※ ※

Shabbos was over, and the air was cool and crisp. It would have been the perfect night for a walk along the broad sidewalks of Grandridge. Often Ezra and Devorah would take to the streets to enjoy the mild caress of a fresh breeze as it brushed their faces. But ordinary activities had taken on intimidating dimensions, blowing away the carefree wind that had once carried them along.

Staying indoors with immediate family was a worthwhile compromise, though.

"Don't be ridiculous!" Ima said in an exasperated tone when she realized her husband was serious about his idea that all of them go on a cruise together. "It's totally irresponsible."

"What's irresponsible about it?" Abba challenged, drying the dish his wife had handed to him. "It's all in your mind. What's the difference between living on a ship and living on dry ground? A ship has all the conveniences you could need or want — it just happens to float on water. Look at it like a mini continent. Right now you live on a continent, right? Well, a continent is surrounded by water, but you don't get worried about that!"

Ima responded with something in Yiddish, which Ezra didn't

understand, although it was quite clear that it wasn't glowing praise. Ezra had been quietly sifting through his mail while his parents did the washing up. The bills were still coming at him hard and fast, bypassing the insurance company and zeroing in on his solitary name, advancing past the 120-day warning and emerging from envelopes that grew a little redder each time.

He still had no idea how this was going to be resolved. Kevin had succeeded in pressing his father about it, but there was as yet no response. These things took so long. He still had not told his family about it, although he could tell Devorah suspected something. She knew him too well.

He dreaded having to resort to cold-calling, to the begging so many other families with similar problems had been forced to do. How many letters had he received in the mail, imploring him to dig in his pocket for the plight of his own, yes, admittedly his own, predicament?

There was a shriek of delight, prompting Ezra to look up from the mail to see his wife playing peek-a-boo with Sarah Malka. Lately they had known virtually no other company but their own. Mother and daughter were locked away together in their own world. Ezra wasn't quite sure how he felt about this.

He docked his chin in his clasped hands and closed his eyes. He was under so much pressure he could burst. Who could take the load off of him? His davening was the only thing that allowed him to truly let go without raising any eyebrows. After all, that was what davening was all about. He understood that Hashem was the ultimate security Who could provide him with the comfort he was looking for. He longed for a voice that would tell him, "Don't worry, Ezra. Don't worry."

*   *   *

Kevin's engagement party had been scheduled for months earlier, but getting everyone in both families to agree on a convenient date was like trying to nab a mosquito in the dark. The party was without a doubt a downscaled version of the grand affair Kevin's father had envisioned. Nevertheless, Ezra could see he was beaming, exceedingly proud of his son who had somehow managed to grow up and reach this point in spite of the upbringing he had been provided.

At first Kevin's father had been suspicious of this little religious stint, but instead of witnessing a shift to radicalism and instability, he had noticed the exact opposite effect — a stabilizing, wholesome calmness that rooted his son. Well, as long as he was happy. And his future daughter-in-law seemed a fine young woman. So who was he to complain?

Ezra leaned against a pillar, sipping a soda and studying the other guests. People chatted in a hyper hum, sprinkling their words with jerky squeals of laughter. The *chasan* and *kallah* stood together by the head table like mannequins, ignoring the piles of cake and fruit laid out in front of them. The food may as well have been plastic, Ezra thought. It was there so that the happy couple could look back at the pictures one day and relish the food that they could have eaten had they not been so utterly, heart-stoppingly nervous. It reminded him of his own engagement party, as these occasions always did. He remembered standing in almost the exact same posture as Kevin — stiff as a stick, with a smile that looked unmistakably bought.

Of course, he could not stave off the pang that besieged him now every time he compared two starkly contrasting points in his life — then and now.

Devorah had planned to join him at the party. Even though the idea of mingling with a crowd had intimidated her, she had insisted on it, part of a newly conceived determination to rejoin the event circuit. But in the last couple of days she had become overly tired and weak and could not leave her bed for very long. This naturally worried everyone no end. They would take her in the following day.

Kevin's father slid over to Ezra, who straightened up as he saw him approach.

"I believe you are Ezra Gelb," he said with a distinctly alcoholic tang.

"Yes, that's right. It's a pleasure to meet you," Ezra responded cordially. "*Mazel tov!*" He extended his hand.

Kevin's father took a backswing to grab at his hand. "Thank you, thank you. You know, I should tell you, I nailed them today."

"Er...excuse me?"

"That's right. I had them practically on their knees on our fluffy green carpet, begging for mercy."

Ezra nodded slowly, thinking he had underestimated just to what extent this man had ventured into liquid la-la land.

"You do know that I'm referring to the insurance, right?" the older man inquired, scrutinizing Ezra's face.

Ezra gasped. "No, I...er...what!"

The man laughed, taking great pleasure in this sweet moment of deliverance he had so valiantly provided. "That's right. They vowed to correct their most unfortunate mistake, and they will begin to make payments as of yesterday."

Ezra couldn't stop himself. He grabbed the other man's hand and thanked him profusely. Indescribable relief rushed in. It felt as if he had been plucked from the grip of quicksand just before he went under. He could finally stand up and dust himself off, his financial burdens lifted. How could he repay Kevin or his father for this? He wanted to share this news with someone, but there was no one else to share it with. As far as the world knew, there never had been a problem in the first place.

His cell phone rang. He hurried out of the room, away from the noise, and answered it.

"Ezra," Ima said. Her voice was edgy, but she spoke slowly. "I...we noticed that Devorah was bleeding a little. So we called the ambulance."

He blinked his eyes, shutting out the stars floating around him. This was way too much. He couldn't take it anymore. *Why? Why? Why?* In his mind he stomped around, kicking and screaming. *Let me out of here! I can't do this. I can't do this.*

There were two other people standing on the balcony, their hands folded over the railing, talking about something probably so frivolous and insipid it made him sick. The drink he had downed earlier turned into an acrid sting inside his body, sending him into a noxious tirade of unrestrained words, feelings, and images all snowballing into something so utterly debilitating it knocked down his usual defenses. His heart had shattered. He was giving up.

He fell back against the railing and sank to the floor, unable and unwilling to move.

11

The Fire

Danny continued to pound on the locked door, even though the noise he produced was an infinitesimal tapping relative to the roar that engulfed him. Eventually he slumped against the door, exhausted, trying to breathe through his sobs. He got onto his knees and began to crawl along the wall, squeezing himself against it. He wanted to look up to check if the monster had spotted him, but he could not bring himself to do it. He just kept crawling along the wall in search of an escape.

Would he wake up now, as he did in those hall-with-no-exit dreams? This didn't feel like a dream, although it was hard to tell. The whole scene had taken on an unreal quality.

He brushed against something. He slid his fingers along the length of it. It was a window with bars like the basement window of his old house. He would often stand on the strip of gravel along the outside wall of the house and peer down through the window into the basement. He would feel like an adult for a moment, looking down at the ground from that elevated vantage point. From there he towered over the tabletops and bookcases that would ordinarily tower over him. He would speak with a deep voice and try to imitate the mundane jargon of adults.

Danny grabbed the bars so he could stare through them, and the grate swung loose, exposing a long narrow chute. He crouched, facing the chute, paralyzed with fear. He didn't know which would be worse — to face the monster or to dive down this corridor.

He chose the latter. At least the corridor would allow him to escape from that terrifying room.

He gave one last wide-eyed look over his shoulder and climbed into the square hole. He could barely fit inside it. He began crawling slowly along the slippery, uneven surface. It was filled with cobwebs, but that didn't scare him. They had always been part of the décor in his daring excursions.

Once, the day after he'd explored the toolshed of an elderly neighbor in the city, he had awoken with a long red line snaking its way up his arm toward his chest. He had pointed it out to his mother with the casualness of a "Look, Mommy." His mother's response had been somewhat more vigorous, and he had wound up in the emergency room before he could complete his presentation.

The noise decreased as he crept further along, and although it was getting darker and his heart was still pounding, it thumped to a different beat, one that was tinged with the excitement of exploration and discovery, the thrill of the genuinely unknown, the wonder of the never-ending passageway springing to life far beyond his makeshift backyard fantasies. This in spite of the fact that he had no idea where he was, in spite of the fact that he didn't know how he was going to get home, in spite of the fact that he really wanted his mommy.

The floor of the tunnel started to slope suddenly, and he lost his grip. He began to slide forward. He tried to grab at the walls, but he caught his fingernail on a sharp edge and yelped with pain as his nail tore. He was now falling at a clip. He could only clench his finger and shut his eyes as he tumbled down the chute, bumping and scraping himself at every twist and turn. He was sure he was falling right into the hands of the monster.

His scream was abruptly halted when he crashed through the grate at the bottom. He landed squarely on his back, the wind knocked out of him. He thought he was dead. His father had told him dying means a person doesn't breathe anymore. Above him the sky was a clear blue, except for a wisp of cloud here and there. His *tatty* always pointed upward when he talked about *Shamayim*.

He waited there on the floor for Hashem to pick him up and take him to *Shamayim*, but he began to breathe again, dissolving any Heavenly expectations. He sat up, ignoring his pain and the moist, raw scrapes that glistened in the sun. There was no roof over his head, but the ground he was sitting on was concrete.

He looked around. He was surrounded by walls of earth. He had made it outside, but he was not quite on ground level. He hobbled slowly over to where the concrete met the steep walls of jagged earth and stared up. He could see the top. Perhaps he could climb out. He inserted his dirt-covered shoe into a hollow in the soil, but it was dry and crumbled as soon as he put any pressure on it. The panic that had subsided when he'd escaped the monster's house now resettled on him with all its initial vigor.

Danny spun around to confirm that he was trapped. He couldn't see past the two gigantic concrete structures that stood in the center of this courtyard. His eyes followed the spiraling concrete upward to where it met the sky. And there he saw, to his horror, that smoke was billowing out of these towers in clouds as thick as the pillars that buttressed his old school office building.

Fire!

He sprinted past the towers to the other side. There the walls of earth were equally as high. Then he scanned the side of the building from which he had emerged. There was a door there. His spirits lifted. He raced to the door and pulled on the rusty handle. It was locked. He stood back against the door and stared at the smoke pouring into the sky. He became aware that his own tears had blurred his vision. He jabbed a filthy hand at his eyes, but that only made it worse. The tears streamed down his face, gathering the sediments of dirt on his skin and carrying them into his mouth.

Please, I want to wake up.

His cries intensified until his voice became hoarse and his screams were rasped, until the sun set on him and he grew still.

🌿 🌿 🌿

"...probably forgotten that the ex-husband took him for the weekend."

"Yeah. Don't joke, man. That actually happened to me once. This woman forgot her son was with his father, and she had the whole police force looking for him. She was so embarrassed she offered to pay us for our trouble."

"Yeah?"

"Yeah."

"So did you take the money?"

"Nah. Didn't feel right."

"Aw, c'mon, man. If I had been there, I would have..."

"Done the exact same thing."

Danny heard them chuckle as he watched the flashlights scour the sky and intersect each other above him. Who were these people?

"DANNY!" one of the voices yelled in no particular direction.

They were calling his name. He stood up, trembling, and answered softly.

"Did you hear that?" one said urgently, stopping in his tracks.

Both voices called out in unison, their mission suddenly turned more serious than they had anticipated.

An arc of light sailed over the small cliff onto the concrete floor where Danny was standing and then flashed clean over his form. It quickly retraced its path and locked onto his face. Danny turned his face away from the blinding glare.

"Man, it's him! He's down there!"

Naturally everyone's relief knew no bounds. Danny's parents showered him with affection and attention, the intensity of which could only be stirred by such a close encounter. This initial euphoria died down over the next few days, uncovering a host of other, more permanent sentiments that rose to the surface, threatening to spill over.

※ ※ ※

Rachel stared at her son from the dining room. He was sitting on the couch, gazing straight ahead, hardly moving, hardly talking. He would not do anything these days that required energy or focus. The most animated activity he would permit himself was playing with the rug tassels or flipping his Rebbe cards. He was so far away. The utter anguish she had felt that horrible day when he was lost had never left her. It had taken up residence in the depths of her soul, where it spilled tears no one could see or touch. She had not lost her son. They had found him. But she felt like she was still in the process of losing him.

Why was he so far away? Where was he that she couldn't reach him? How could she strip away the layers that had surreptitiously distanced her from him?

"Danny?" she said softly.

He turned to look at her with hollow eyes. It scared her. Rachel backed out of the room and returned to the kitchen. That was it. She refused to treat this as a passing phase, as much as Menachem preferred to avoid facing a reality that was different from his image of a picture-perfect family. Something was wrong, and she was going to do something about it.

12

Ezra and Dr. Harding sat a couple seats down from where a man slept fitfully across three or four chairs. Apart from them, the waiting room was empty. The air was a little murky, saturated with stale cigarette smoke that someone had guiltily produced when no one was looking. Ezra leaned back in his chair, his hands gripping the edges of his seat.

"I think it is definitely possible to go ahead with another chemo," the doctor was saying. "Mrs. Gelb showed a remarkable return to strength during her remission. I think it is safe for us to proceed, and hopefully we will see her back in remission after this treatment."

The doctor's sallow glumness was in full force. His face was so yellow it was almost luminous. He was truly a chameleon, his skin blending in with his mood, with his heart. A more compassionate physician Ezra had never encountered. Even the way he spoke was soothing and gentle, smoothing over the rough edges of the disturbing information he was imparting.

Ezra nodded. There was nothing really to say except "Thank you, doctor."

The doctor lifted his eyebrows in response and rose to leave. "All the best."

Ezra needed the *Tehillim*. He returned to Devorah's room, the very same room Devorah had stayed in before. The familiarity was both comforting and disturbing. Devorah found it comforting; Ezra found it disturbing. The previous time her wall had been lined with Sarah Malka's colorful "I love you, Mommy" posters produced by proxy. Now Devorah insisted that they be retrieved from the box in the garage and affixed in their exact positions. Everything, from her clothing to her medication, had to be returned to their previous arrangement.

Ezra knew she craved permanence. That was how she functioned. She was always looking to order things around her like the flashing lights of a cockpit's controls so she could establish her bearings and direct her thoughts to where they needed to go. She had obviously cultivated a certain approach to her illness during her previous stay in the hospital, and she wanted to latch on to that again.

Ezra, on the other hand, had the unnerving sensation that he was revisiting the past. He preferred to look at things as a progression. It was the same feeling he had when he had returned to school for a programming course several years after graduating. Walking down the halls, sitting in the classrooms, raising his hand, he hadn't been able to suppress the sensation that he had regressed.

Ima was tending to the baby at home. Sarah Malka had caught a cold, and it was not a good idea to bring her into the hospital.

Devorah was looking out the window. Her eyes were only half open, and Ezra couldn't tell if she was looking at the fading sunlight and gently waving trees or if she was lost in thought. It was also possible that she was merely dizzy and disoriented. This had become more common in the last few days.

"Devorah?"

She turned her head slowly to face him.

"I was just thinking about the baby's teeth in the pillows," she said softly.

He stared at her. Her eyes were blank and bleary. She returned her attention to the window. Her head shook as if her slackened neck muscles couldn't hold it up. The room was quiet except for his own strained breathing. He was trying to fight back tears. His wife, his best friend in the whole world, his companion in conversation for all of life's encounters, from the most dreary and mundane to the most vital and spectacular, was losing her ability to talk to him.

After a while, he sat down, resting his head on his clasped hands and fixing his eyes on Devorah. He continued to sit there and stare in the agonizing silence until Ima relieved him hours later.

The cookies seemed rounder and plumper this time. Ezra could tell that Mrs. Zimmerman had doused them with extra care and affection. The whole town was mired in the gloom of Devorah's relapse. Still, Aryeh believed that sympathy was not what Ezra needed, and the truth was Ezra was not looking for it either. He needed direction, perspective, something solid to take home with him. He needed something he could etch into the fibers of his senses so that when he breathed, spoke, or listened it would reverberate with utter clarity.

Even so, Ezra would never give the impression that he was looking for anything. He would sit there, forlorn and despondent, not to mention slightly annoyed. And then Aryeh would say something. He had that knack. Many times it was an astounding insight that provided pristine clarity. But it wasn't always something new. It was the way it was said, or when it was said, that never failed to turn it around for Ezra.

Aryeh regarded these encounters with trepidation, swallowing nervously as he invited Ezra in. He had enormous expectations to live up to. He would close his eyes and daven a blitz of a prayer, every nanosecond of it a petition for volumes of Heavenly assistance. And then they would both sit down together and face the cookie stand-off.

"I know I'm supposed to believe that things can suddenly turn around with a...what's it called again?"

"*Heref ayin*. A blink of an eye."

"Right. But, Aryeh, I know theoretically that we are required to beseech Hashem with all our hearts even when the prospects are grim. I know theoretically that even when the sword is at one's neck one has to keep on davening. I've probably heard all the stories of how a miracle happens and in the last minute there is a recovery. But it's all theoretical for me.

"When I walk into the ward and pass that chart, I am drawn to the figures and the graphs and what the doctors are saying. Believe me, I don't always believe what they say, but there is a certain heaviness to their words, a certain gravitational pull that tells me to focus on the facts. The miracles are reduced to mere fine print that appear only in books.

"Aryeh, I believe in miracles. I do. I just can't get myself to believe that they can happen to me, that they're just as real as these cookies and this plate and the air I breathe."

He took a breath on the word *breathe*, as if he had suddenly made himself conscious of it.

"And then, of course, we never hear of the stories where a miracle doesn't happen," he added.

Aryeh sighed deeply, puffing out his cheeks, causing his moustache to stretch. "Well, sure, you're not going to see those stories published. Can you imagine? What would you think of a book called *The Miracle That Never Happened?*"

Ezra gave a bittersweet smile. "Well, why not? They should show both sides of the story to be fair, shouldn't they?"

"Ezra, listen to me. We are forever looking at life through pigeon holes. Open up a book of Jewish history and see. You will realize how improbable it is, based on the facts, that we are around today. The persecution, the oppression, the lies, the hatred that still goes on even today would destroy the mightiest of nations in a flash. And here we are, a small stiff-necked people, who get around with a *heimishe* smile and a little bit of *seichel*. And we destroy the hopes of entire nations that are enamored with the concept of a world that is *Judenrein*. No logic can explain it."

The words were rolling off his tongue, and he plowed on, while the inspiration was flowing.

"Do you know what that means for us? It means that by all rights you and I should not be alive. It means that each and every Jew is a living miracle. Our whole essence is a miracle. That is who we are. The rules of normal society, of averages, means, and likelihoods, do not apply to us."

"That would make us invincible and immortal," Ezra interjected. "If we operate on different rules, why do Jews get seriously ill just like non-Jews do?"

"We're human. We are not celestial beings. We function, live, and behave like humans. But, just like every country has its own yardstick for measuring its citizens' behavior, so too the Jewish people have their own yardstick for measuring their behavior. Things happen to Jews just like they happen to non-Jews. The difference is that we do not employ the yardstick of the nations in measuring our hows and whys."

Ezra mulled over these words. This concept alone would have been sufficient to win him over to the cookies. Aryeh's presentation this evening was scintillating.

"What you're saying is that we are not necessarily bound by a certain percentage of cancer patients succumbing to their illnesses per year," Ezra proposed.

Aryeh smiled. "That's right. Of course, that has to be put into perspective. It doesn't guarantee that everything is going to turn out fine. All it means is that someone who is given only a slight chance can — in Jewish reality — have a much greater chance. That does not guarantee the result. But it should change the defeatist frame of mind that is invoked when these percentages and statistics are doled out to you."

Aryeh leaned forward. "Of course, we have to daven for it. Our nation as a whole can rely on the covenant Hashem made with us that He will never destroy us. But as individuals we cannot expect to be dealt with differently if we don't show that we are different."

Ezra stared at the cookies that beckoned to be swooped up and demolished. He was aware that a move toward them would be like crossing the divide, admitting to the truth that was flowing from Aryeh's lips, accepting it in his heart. It would be the mobilization of all his energy toward a hefty challenge, the actualization of this theory of which he had been aware, yet had not made a part of him. He knew the statistics. He knew of the inexplicable phenomenon of Jewish existence. But he had always known it as a distant detail that had never quite made it into his everyday life. When he would stretch out his arm to partake of the food, that would be the moment of acceptance, of the piercing penetration of the theoretical and the intellectual into his living core.

Aryeh stared at him expectantly. It was as if the whole world had stopped and was waiting for him to proceed. Had all this happened to him so he could reach this moment of critical choice?

His hand shot out and grabbed a cookie, and he became a different person.

"I know this seems self-serving," Ezra proclaimed from the podium of the shul. Dozens of eyes stared up at him, captivated by his uncapped gusto. They let him get away with it because it was real. It was as if a line connected the walls of his heart to an amplifier.

"I would never have stood here speaking to you like this, proposing what I am about to propose, had my wife not gotten sick. On the surface, it seems my only motivation to get you to improve yourselves along with me is in order to get my own prayers answered.

"Well, if that's how it seems to you, then I'd say you're right. But you're also wrong. Sometimes it takes a crisis to open up your eyes and trigger a response, and that's not selfish at all. It's hard for me to explain, and, as I've said before, I don't wish any of you to be in my shoes. I do believe that as a result of all of this my relationship with Hashem has grown in leaps and bounds. My insight into life, what is important in life, has matured to an astounding degree.

"I hope you forgive me for what may sound like bragging. Please believe that I have no interest in honor right now. Hashem has caused me to see through the peripherals about which we concern ourselves, the hypnotizing fluff that grabs us. Hashem has made sure that my mind is kept busy focusing on life-and-death matters. When you are living with such concerns uppermost in your mind, your desire for self-aggrandizement takes a very definite back seat.

"The point is, I want to share my excitement with you. It's not like the previous occasion where my objective was a collective effort to bring about what I so desperately needed. This time I am imploring you to realize the importance of serving Hashem for your sakes, too.

"We are about to daven *mussaf*. I ask you to do something that some of you may find...well, a little heavy for a regular Shabbos morning. I ask each and every one of you to picture this *mussaf* as if it were the only *mussaf* you will ever recite in your entire lifetime. There is only one *mussaf*, and today is when you are going to say it. I don't think I need to exhort you to concentrate on each and every word, because I doubt that there is any one of you here who would not pass up such an invaluable opportunity. I do ask that this effort should be in the merit of Devorah Leah bas Rivka, but at the same time I am asking you to do it for yourselves."

This time the air was peppered with a murmur here and a grumble there. It seemed the congregants were not so eager and accommodating as they had been on the previous occasion. Perhaps it was the forcefulness of his delivery, or perhaps you could get away with such an audacious, intrusive request only once. His privileges as an upstanding member of the community could only go so far. Perhaps it was more of a subconscious red flag that shot up at the sound of someone preaching at them, trying to improve them for their sake. It evoked a shield-bearing defense that asserted, "I'm doing just fine, thank you — and anyway who are you to tell me what's good for me?"

Whatever the reason, there were fewer hands extended to him on the way back to his seat, and those who did so seemed reluctant. Ezra was not bothered by this. Ever since that pivotal moment around Aryeh's dining-room table, it seemed a whole panorama of enlightened perspectives had opened up to him. He had become passionate about the reality of Torah, of the Jewish people, of the powerful spiritual denominator bringing together each fold and corner of Jewish survival. It had nothing to do with scoring points for an outreach campaign. It was about imparting to his fellow Jews something he could have learned only from the searing depths of his predicament.

And that was precisely why, when it came to the actual recitation of *mussaf*, the congregants dipped into an intense, heart-stopping roar of commingling voices. The air was electric; faces were taut. It lasted much longer than any other *mussaf* Ezra could recall, and he was heartened by it. It just went to show that when it came down to it they would surrender to the little voice that urged them on to do whatever was right, even if they would not admit it.

Ezra was encouraged to do more. But what else could he do?

Cold-calling. This was something Ezra had never envisioned himself doing. If there was one redeeming feature of the world of computers, it was the fact that it was a haven from social interaction. There was very little that was glossy and glamorous about it, and it required virtually no heart-on-the-sleeve hard selling. He could not imagine having to start the day prepping himself to charm the dollars out of a customer's pocket.

He skipped up the steps at the first address on his contact list. The doorbell awaited his hesitant finger. He reminded himself that he was living up to the salesman's die-hard motto: believe in the product you're selling. He had nothing to fear.

And yet a face muscle twitched and an eyelid fluttered. He found himself silently wishing that Mrs. Melissa Feldman would not be at home.

But she was.

The door swung open and revealed Ezra, a grinning stranger on her doorstep.

"Can I help you?"

"Sure." Ezra swallowed, trying to act as if he was part of the family.

"I'm Ezra and my wife has leukemia." He couldn't stop the words from tumbling out of his mouth. This was certainly not how he had planned it. His cheeks flushed red, and he realized he would immediately have to throw in a disclaimer. "I'm not here for money. I'm here because I am a Jew and you are a Jew, and I want to present you with a package my mother put together."

Aargh! He could not have done it any worse had he tried.

She stared at him with a frown that had etched itself across her forehead. Had it not been for his respectable appearance and the innocence in his voice, she would probably have shut the door on him without a second thought. He dug into a bag of wrapped packages. He presented one to her.

"There are two challos in here, two candles, and a bottle of wine so that you may enjoy a Sabbath meal tonight."

Her face softened. He could tell the sight of the gift had shot arrows of nostalgia into her heart, bringing fond memories of a mother or grandmother gathering the children to light Shabbos candles on the mantelpiece. She even began to smile.

"Are you a rabbi?"

"No. I'm just someone who has realized the importance of rekindling the flame, so to speak."

Mrs. Feldman stood awkwardly against the door. "Could I offer you something to drink, perhaps?"

"No, thank you. All I ask is that you take this gift and use it and perhaps utter a little prayer for the recovery of my wife, Devorah Gelb."

She tilted her head as if pondering something. "You know, I read about you. You've had all those rallies and prayers, am I right?"

Ezra nodded.

Now her face filled with admiration. She looked down at her package and back at him. "This is a very sweet gesture. Thank you."

Ezra skipped back down the steps to his car and drove to the next address. He reviewed his first confrontation, peeling apart each moment like it was film reel. This was painful to do, and he found himself squirming at certain embarrassing points. Well, it just went to show that presentation did not matter in the end. You had to truly want what was best for the person.

*   *   *

Ima was patching together another batch of challah, wine, and candles when Ezra waltzed in all smiles from his successful delivery stint. Her movements were sharp and hurried, and she appeared agitated.

"Ezra, this is the last batch I'm making for you. Tonight is Shabbos, and I still have to get to the hospital. There is no one with Devorah, and the nurses must be wondering why we've abandoned her for so long."

She sealed a package with a piece of tape that had been hanging from her lips. She had not fully understood the change that had come over her son in the last few weeks. It was true he wanted to do mitzvos, and she *shepped* plenty of *nachas* from that. But this was a little over the top.

"Ima, you were at the hospital this morning. You've been away for only two and a half hours."

"Ezra! Two and a half hours is a long time to be alone when you're ill." She returned to her rapid movements, and in the stilted silence that followed Ezra felt the sting of her disappointment.

Sarah Malka broke the ice. Well, not ice exactly, but a wine bottle that had been inadvertently placed next to her on the floor for want of table space. She was drenched in red and surrounded by a litter of tiny glass fragments. Just at that point the doorbell rang. Of course.

"I'll get it!" Abba yelled from the living room where he had been napping until the commotion in the kitchen had jolted him awake. It was Arthur from the shul board with a petition that expressed utter dissatisfaction with the current board and proposed their entire dismissal and the scheduling of new elections as soon as possible. He needed to speak with Ezra about it at great length.

And so this particular Friday afternoon would not disappoint in developing into the frenetic chaos that was typical of most Friday afternoons as the day of bliss and tranquility approached.

※ ※ ※

Car lights from the distant freeway flickered as they passed through the treetops. A slow drizzle soaked the ground, trees, and air. Ezra stared at this sight from the window of the hospital room. His thoughts swirled with the rain and the fog, twisting in and out of the trees and blurring with the lamplight reflected in the window.

Devorah was asleep. Her breathing was gentle and calm, a total contrast to the wired bundle of nerves that sparked through everyone else in the room. Devorah's mother chewed on her nails, a habit she continually battled, especially after an expensive manicure like this one, which she had just received on their little Italian getaway last week. Devorah's father paced the room, a hand in his pocket, the other stroking his chin. Ima was checking the IV yet again, and Abba was trying to distract Sarah Malka and himself with a spontaneous flick-the-matchstick game.

Ima eyed her husband. "After all these years, Abe, you still haven't learned that children shouldn't play with matches." Her voice crackled through the hollow air.

"People are overly protective when it comes to these things. They worry about the possible harmful effects of playing with matches, but they don't worry about the definite harmful effects of plunking their kids in front of a TV set."

Ezra smiled. He had always admired his father's humble way of imparting wisdom. Only in an inane moment like this would he let it spill out. These remarks always caught Ima off guard, though. She would either laugh or put an abrupt halt to her end of the conversation.

Finally Dr. Harding walked into the room. Ezra felt the heat of anticipation rise up through him, inflaming his senses until they pounded with trepidation. All eyes were on the doctor. But his eyes were not on them. There was no twinkle in them either. His face was ashen.

Ezra began to quiver as the blood drained out of him. His eyes nose-dived to the ground, like a plane out of control. Everyone there understood. The doctor did not have to explain.

He did anyway.

"Hardly any impression was made on the cancer cells in this last treatment. I'm sorry." He stood still, his chin tucked into his chest and his deep frown bearing the brunt of his own words.

Please, don't say there's nothing more we can do, Ezra silently pleaded. Though he realized that this was exactly what the doctor was saying, he felt that not voicing the actual words would keep it from becoming official, signed and sealed.

"I'm sorry," the doctor repeated.

Ima excused herself. Devorah's mother buried her head in her hands. Devorah's father collapsed into a chair as if his legs could no longer hold him up. Abba put down the baby and went over to Ezra. They hugged each other for a very long time, both of them brimming with tears. The doctor continued to stand in his spot, sharing in the sorrow as part of his personal catharsis, his need to be a part of the suffering he had failed to alleviate.

Ezra withdrew from his father's embrace and wiped away his tears. His mind had begun to fill with the knowledge he had learned, the reality he had ingested and integrated into the fibers of his being. It breathed fresh hope into his senses, helping him to cling stubbornly to the tightrope of life. *We are not necessarily bound by numbers and predictions.*

"Doctor," he said, clearing his throat, "are there any other alternatives we can explore?"

Dr. Harding looked up. "Well, there are always new drugs being tested. I know that there are certain circumstances such as this, when the conventional methods of treatment have been exhausted, that you may get permission to use them."

Ezra's eyes widened. "Can you tell me more?"

"Unfortunately, I don't know much more." He shrugged. "I do know that there has been some success with a drug used to treat CML. But Mrs. Gelb has AML, and for that I have not heard about any substantive results. Research is continually being done in this area."

Ezra wrung his hands, his eyes darting back and forth, trying to keep up with the rapid firing of his thoughts.

The first thing that came to mind was the Internet. He glanced at his watch. The office was already closed. He would have to get the key from Kevin so he could use the company computer. He had to get to work on this right away.

He made a break for the door, so keenly focused that he managed only a half-mumble in explanation as he whizzed past everyone to get to the elevators.

※ ※ ※

The dark lobby was haunting in its glaring absence of people. He had never been there at this time of night. It was even past leaving time for the incurable workaholics who always stayed late, hunching over their desks with bleary eyes.

The computer whirred loudly in the silence as he clicked it on, the sound usually drowned out by a constant hum of activity. Now it was magnified, taking center stage, resounding through the office and bounding over the empty chairs and desks.

He and Devorah were opposed to having the Internet at home because of its disconcerting resemblance to television. Even if it were possible to avoid all that was unsavory, it still lured its viewer away from normal life for countless hours of that mindless activity called "surfing," which gave the impression of doing something, clicking ahead to a more progressive destination. But it had its uses.

He logged onto a search engine, and instantly he was provided with a wealth of information. There were articles, studies, institutes, and links that told him he was not the first one to explore this topic. He had tapped into a whole network of people like him, searching and digging up every inch of on-line territory in the hope of striking medicinal gold that no one had heard of before, that was on the brink of revolutionizing the world of oncology.

The night ticked away as he scanned hundreds of attractive alternatives. There was so much to investigate he didn't know where to begin. There were biological and pharmacological therapies, which involved deriving nontoxic medication from biological sources. An example of this was the use of amino acids to inhibit the growth of cancer cells. There were immunological therapies, which prescribed the use of vaccines to bolster the immune system. Ezra was unsure how affective this would be at Devorah's stage. There were herbal therapies, metabolic therapies, and even mind-body therapies.

But what drew his attention the most was the ongoing clinical studies listed around the country. Site after site detailed very specific requirements for patients wishing to enter a study. Ezra didn't understand much of the jargon, but what he got out of it was that there were a lot of options. There was so much going on. He wanted to dive in head first.

He glanced at his watch and received a mild shock. It was three in the morning. But he wasn't tired at all. He was invigorated, anxious to try everything that was available.

Aryeh's words rushed through his head. The trick was remembering the reality, that which lay behind the veil of day-to-day normality. Ignore the predictions and percentages. We are not necessarily bound by them. He had succeeded thus far in bolstering himself with this deep knowledge, incorporating it into his struggles. Now he had to surge forward with these therapies and trials. There was hardly a moment to lose.

🌿 🌿 🌿

This time Devorah's homecoming was shrouded in darkness, an overwhelming despair that pervaded every room of the house. She herself was only vaguely aware of her homecoming, the images of hospital and home merging to form one distorted picture that blanked out now and then when her eyes would shut involuntarily. Her face was pale and expressionless, accepting every passing second with the innocence of a baby wrapped up in his own world, oblivious to his surroundings.

There was a noticeable slowing in Ima's efforts. Instead of whispering words of encouragement in her daughter-in-law's ears as she busily adjusted, folded, filled, and emptied, she sat silently by Devorah's side, getting up only to perform the most basic of necessities. More than once Ezra noticed her staring uncharacteristically ahead, her eyes glazed over. He knew that her hope had begun to dissolve, that she had begun to resign herself to a fate more horrible than she could imagine. She now made less use of her sunglasses, dropping all pretexts and crying openly into the palms of her hands.

All her life she had longed for a daughter, a dream that had been fulfilled in a way she had not expected, through one woman's magical bond with her own precious son. She had been sold on their first meeting when Devorah had smiled nervously at her on the doorstep. From then on it had grown into an inseparable friendship that struck roots so deep that it became difficult to imagine there had ever been a time that they had not known each other. It seemed they shared the same blood, pulsing with a mutual affection that was hard to mimic even in the strongest of mother-daughter relationships.

And now she was looking at a future that seemed frightening and disorienting, sure she was being sent reeling into a lost world.

Abba had also become more distant, spending more time attending to the baby, who would not be snatched from him. He took care of her every need, be it food, diaper changes, or rounds of peek-a-boo.

Only Ezra remained charged by his convictions, still running on his current of ideals and mental tools. He had hardly gotten any sleep in his recent pursuit of clinical trials for Devorah. He spent his days calling, meeting, e-mailing, and researching. He rarely showed up for work, staying only a couple of hours at most. He was surely going to lose his job. There was only so much he could expect them to tolerate.

He would not have minded had at least some progress been made. But he had hit a wall when it came to signing the consent forms to participate in the trials. Devorah was required to do it, and Ezra doubted she would be able to. There were other factors, each trial encumbered by their own special requirements. But this was the main one. Devorah did have her lucid moments, but he doubted he would be able to coordinate it properly.

One evening, after pounding away at the office keyboard, he returned home to find Ima fast asleep in her chair next to Devorah's bed, her face turned into the nook of the chair back. Devorah was wide awake, sitting up. Her eyes were not rolling as they had begun to do in the last few days. They seemed steady and focused.

"Hi," she said, smiling, in a voice that was a flashback to the past.

"Hi," he croaked, suddenly nervous. It was like he had to reintroduce himself.

"Ezra, I want you to promise me something."

He swallowed, his hands gripping the back of Ima's chair.

"I want you to promise me that you will get remarried." Devorah paused, showing no trace of emotion, as if she was on strictly official orders.

Ezra went pale. "Devorah, please don't talk like that."

"Ezra, I want you to promise me."

This surely ranked up there with the most uncomfortable moments in his life. He could not look at her. How could she expect him to fulfill such a request? He felt anger rising up, but it quickly turned to stirrings of admiration. He knew she was saying this solely for his benefit, that he should know that she herself had sanctioned his getting on with his life after... But no, he refused to be drawn into a defeatist outlook on the future.

"Devorah, there's still hope. I'm working on getting into clinical trials, and today I got some promising information on two herbal formulas that have shown good results."

He spoke quickly, feeling as if he had to cram all that he was doing into this tiny window of lucidity. But halfway through his words, her eyelids had begun to droop, and she lost focus, turning her head toward the window, staring at nothing in particular.

His words petered out. It was like they had lost radio contact, and all he could do was stare at her through opaque glass. His mind swirled with her request, numbing his senses.

"I promise," he whispered, his voice breaking up.

It was the hardest thing he had ever had to say. But if that was what Devorah wanted, he wasn't going to deny her. He would never know whether she had heard him or not, but at least he had said the words.

※ ※ ※

After scaling a daunting mountain of paperwork and bureaucracy, it looked like Ezra was finally able to secure an opening for Devorah to be a part of a clinical trial for an AML-targeting drug. It would mean transporting her to the particular cancer institute involved, but it was only an hour away. It was certainly worth a try.

Ima agreed that this was a necessary step. At once she began making preparations, though the trial was scheduled for two weeks' time. Ezra was glad to see her rising somewhat from her lethargy. Perhaps a sliver of hope had found its way inside her. At least it gave her direction and a distraction from the grim thoughts that filled her mind recently.

But it was a calm Sunday morning, a week until the trials, that everyone had somehow known to file into the bedroom and to take their seats beside Devorah's bed. Her eyes were closed, her breathing slow and heavy, her hands icy to the touch. Ima tried to rub some warmth into them, but the coldness was deep and inaccessible.

No one said a word. Ezra sat slumped in his chair, his hair a cropped mess and his face craggy and dried-up. He looked at least twenty years older than he was. Just the other day a visiting nurse had asked him if he was Devorah's father. Ima said the nurse had obviously been hallucinating, but after that Ezra had made sure to stop in front of a mirror for the first time in a very long while. The image that greeted him shocked him. He hardly recognized the withered shell that held his face. At the same time, he was fascinated by how much of a pounding his body could take and still manage to function.

A thick pillar of sunlight poured through the window, illuminating the soft threads of Devorah's woolen blanket. Sarah Malka was asleep in her infant seat alongside the bed, her gentle snores overshadowed by her mother's more labored breathing. There was no other sound as everyone looked on with unwavering intensity.

Ezra sat forward as he traced the lines on his wife's face with his eyes. He felt a strange undercurrent of energy running through the room. It was not an uncomfortable sensation, rather a type of warmth that permeated him and spread through him.

Just then Devorah lifted her arms straight above her as if to take hold of something. Just as quickly, her arms collapsed at her sides. She breathed her last breath, and her soul slipped out of her, the warmth in the room swelling to a glowing fire, delaying the onset of the terrible void that was knocking on the doors, pressing to swoop in and devour everything in its path.

13

The Other Side of the Farm

Dr. Ellen Granovich had a cold stare that pierced through surfaces, organic or inorganic, with the sharpness of frozen needles. Yet when she opened her mouth to speak, her voice was as flat as a history lecturer's, dragging out each word to produce a low drone. This, together with the half-closed blinds that dimmed the light and the soft puffy chairs, left Danny's parents battling to stay awake. It seemed that the task of investigating and treating the mind was facilitated by dulling the sensory preceptors so that all else would dissolve and fizz out.

Danny's legs hung off his chair. He kicked them as he watched the lady speak, his eyelids feeling heavy. He had no idea that this session largely centered around him. As far as he knew, this was just another uneventful stop on the boring adult ride, like the long hours waiting on line at the bank or the trips to the post office and supermarket that astonishingly adults chose to endure.

Then the lady turned to him and smiled. He did not smile back.

"Danny, do you know my name?" She took out a piece of construction paper and some crayons and began to draw with sweeping strokes.

His legs stopped kicking. He watched her with eagle eyes, his mouth hanging open.

She raised her picture and flashed it proudly in front of him. "You see, this is me. Ellen."

She pointed to the squiggly stick figure with an oversize head and a half-moon smile.

Danny nodded shyly.

She withdrew from her desk a pile of thick paper and cardboard of a wide variety of shapes and colors, followed by a large assortment of the longest and thickest crayons Danny had ever seen. As she was doing this, she pursed her lips and raised her eyebrows up high, as if to relay to him the monumental significance of this task.

She got up from behind her desk, sat down on the floor beside it, and spread out all the materials.

"Do you think you would be able to draw a picture of yourself, Danny?"

She waited there without looking at him, thumbing the edges of a spectacular slice of glittered cardboard.

Danny looked at his parents. They smiled at him. They seemed just as enchanted as he was.

He got up slowly and joined Dr. Granovich on the floor. His

eye caught on a silver crayon that was as thick as a Popsicle. He grabbed it, aimed it at a vast sheet of pitch-black cardboard, glanced one more time at his parents, and got to work.

🌿 🌿 🌿

The drive back and forth from Dr. Granovich's office was always filled with anxiety. Apart from the fact that this was precious time that Menachem had to find from a very hectic work schedule, there was also the eeriness of emerging afterward from a very personal mental surgery. It seemed that the doctor always left her mind scalpel wedged in their personas, deliberately refraining from sewing up the incisions. This annoyed Menachem, who was still not at all sure there was something wrong in the first place. As for Rachel, the stigma of being treated as mental patients only served to endorse her vote of no confidence in her parental capabilities.

Ironically Danny enjoyed the visits, which were always filled with exciting activities. Rachel had to admit that he had started showing some improvement at home. He was talking more and had shown a greater interest in doing things rather than just sitting on the couch. But he was still wetting his bed, and he still shied away from his peers at school. There was definitely still a lot of ground to cover.

This was exactly why Dr. Granovich, at the end of one session, announced to Danny's parents that the time had come to try something new. It was true the monsters were now openly depicted all over a multicolored jumble of paper and cardboard, and that

Danny was slowly learning to confront them, be it in reality, illusion, or the gray area in-between. It was true he and Dr. Granovich were talking about the monsters constantly, like they were part of the family, part of the sleepy furniture in the office. But he still showed signs of post-traumatic stress disorder, apparently resulting from his vague experiences with these monsters and the farm next door.

"I think this may be a good time to explore EMDR," Dr. Granovich suggested in her usual low monotone.

"What's that?" Rachel sat forward, her head filling with visions of CAT scans, EEGs, operating rooms, and buzzing electrodes in dark rooms.

"Well," the doctor continued, in no apparent rush to placate her, "EMDR is short for eye movement desensitization and reprocessing. It is an increasingly popular technique that integrates many different orientations to treat a particular traumatic event."

"Do you think my son has been traumatized?" Menachem interjected, his frown rigid and unrelenting.

"It's difficult to classify it with certainty at this stage. But even if we are not comfortable with the term *trauma*, we can be sure that this technique would be effective for any stress, since studies have proved its effectiveness with genuinely traumatic cases."

She gave him a smile, as if to assert, "Work with me, not against me."

She continued her explanation, her words seeping out of her mouth with all the urgency of a Sunday afternoon tea party.

"In this process, a light is waved in front of the patient. The patient follows the light with his eyes as it moves, at the same time focusing on the issue that is causing the trauma."

Danny's parents looked at each other. Even Danny's mother, who up to this point had held the doctor in high esteem, was astounded. It sounded ridiculous.

The doctor continued to speak, but they just stared right through her to her wall and her mahogany-framed certificates. Finally she revealed that she was not trained in this area and would have to refer them to another therapist who was an expert in it.

Nevertheless, the doctor was no fool, and she began rattling off, in her own sluggish way, an infinite number of case studies that seemed to provide indisputable proof of the magical efficacy of this method. She went on and on, until Danny's mother was convinced that it was worth a try.

Their enchantment with this method began to wear off the moment they left the office. It was probably the effect of emerging from that fuzzy enclave and facing the dry reality of the outside world. Doubts crept up on Rachel all the way to the car, all through the drive home, and up to the moment she lay in bed that night wide awake. She tried to immerse herself in a biography she had started, but it wasn't grabbing her. Instead, a foreboding picture of a pendulum-dangling hypnotist presented itself in her mind. It was like trying not to think of pink elephants. It was there to stay much throughout the night — until her thoughts were suddenly halted by a bloodcurdling scream.

Both parents bolted to their son's room. They turned on the light. Danny lay there, half asleep, writhing, embroiled in yet another phantom struggle with the enemy. The noise woke Yosef.

"That's it!" Rachel declared, lifting her son out of his bed. Her husband thought she was heading for the rocking chair, where she would typically hold him until his cries subsided. But this time she opened the closet to search out some clothes for him.

"What are you doing?" Menachem asked, blinking the sleep out of his red eyes.

"Menachem, I'm sorry, but I should have done this in the first place," she said, pulling off Danny's pajama top. "I'm taking him to the baker."

"What!"

"I know it seems ridiculous. It's the middle of the night. But he's the only one who really seems to understand Danny. Every time I've taken him there, he's come out much happier. I don't know what it is, but he has a way with Danny. I just know he would be willing to help us."

"But...how...what?..."

"Menachem, I can't let this go on." Rachel stopped midway through fastening a shirt button. She turned around to face him, biting her lip. "I don't know what's happening to our little boy." Her voice was soft and faltering, and she was trying to hold back her tears. "I...I don't think I want to subject him to some hypnotic trance."

Menachem stood still, his head bowed. She could see this was one of those rare occasions where he gave himself permission to acknowledge the severity of a problem.

"We should call him first," he said finally. "We shouldn't show up at his doorstep in the middle of the night without warning."

"Okay." She smiled. "His home number is in the shul phone book."

※ ※ ※

The lights were on in the baker's home when they pulled up. There was a stiff breeze brushing the trees and beating at their coats. Something was brewing on Grandridge's varied weather menu.

The door opened to the welcoming whiff of steaming coffee.

"Thank you so much for letting us disturb you like this in the middle of the night, Mr. Zimmerman. I can't tell you how much we appreciate it." Danny's mother smiled gratefully as she removed her coat.

"Please, please," he said, flapping his hand. "First of all, you can call me Aryeh. And you're not disturbing me. Believe it or not, I was just getting up as you called. Bakers have to get a very early start, you know."

They all moved to the dining-room table, where Mrs. Zimmerman had already set out a plate of cookies.

"These look great, Mrs. Zimmerman," Menachem called out, handing one to Danny, whose bloodshot eyes cleared upon sight of the baker and the cookies.

"You know, she's a far better baker than I am," Aryeh declared, loud enough for his wife to hear. "How do you think I learned to bake?" He laughed, his moustache alternately flexing and bunching.

Danny's mother updated Aryeh on all that was going on. Her eyes darted now and then to her husband to check if she was disclosing anything too personal. But he sat back in his chair, expressionless, apparently resigned to whatever was necessary to get this solved.

Aryeh turned to look at Danny, who was munching merrily away at his cookie as if it was all that existed in the world.

"Danny, did you see the monster again?"

Danny glanced up at him, wiping the crumbs from his mouth. He smiled nervously.

"I saw his house," he said.

His parents were stunned. This was the first time they had heard this. There was obviously a unique language that existed between the two of them, the baker and their son.

"What did it look like?"

Danny's eyes swelled in anticipation of his own elaborate descriptions. He told of the giant room with the mysterious hidden passages, the locked door, the thunderous metal jaws that crushed the food from the field...

The field. Aryeh's mind began to do flips with this clue. Image after image was jumbled, sorted, and fused together to form a composite picture that expanded exponentially. A grass-eating monster, a field, a building with grinding metal... It had to be. The chills running up his spine locked him in his seat, his stare frozen and his breathing arrested.

Finally he turned to the curious parents. "The field he is describing, is that Pat Johnson's wheat farm?"

"I...don't know the name of the owner," Rachel stammered. "But, yes, it's a wheat farm. Right next door."

Aryeh swung his head back in Danny's direction.

"Danny, do you know what a farm is?"

"Yeah."

"Tell me, what is it?"

"It's got animals in it."

Aryeh's mind raced ahead at lightning speed, fuses spitting and wires sparking. He jumped from his seat and headed for an old, warped bookcase. He withdrew a large, thick volume and returned to the table. Everyone, including Mrs. Zimmerman from behind him, watched with fascination as he fumbled through the encyclopedia until he came to a page that prompted him to cry, "Aha!"

Everyone craned their necks to see. A picture of a wheat farm headed the entry. Just below it was nothing other than the elusive, deceptive, trouble-stirring monster — the tractor. Danny shrank back in fright, but then crept back up to give it another look. His mother recalled that right in the beginning she had suggested the monster may have been a tractor, and her son had rejected it. How foolish she had been for not pursuing it further. Once again, she could feel the tug of those ever-present guilt strings.

Aryeh proceeded to explain to Danny all about the farming process, how the tractor, the larger combine harvester that came after it, and the flour mill were, believe it or not, there to help us. All these things were used to produce a very valuable end product. But he stopped there. He would not reveal what this end product was.

He decided it would be most effective to witness the results in practice.

And so everyone piled into their respective cars and sped off to the bakery, just when an early-morning drizzle had begun to turn into freezing rain. There they munched on some of the previous day's pickings while Aryeh disappeared into the back to get the oven going.

After a while, he reappeared and gestured for Danny to follow him into the back. Danny jumped at the opportunity. He had always wondered what lay back there.

What he saw unsettled him. Had the baker not accompanied him there, he would have been, well...afraid. This room was much smaller than the building on the farm, but it, too, was cluttered with lots of menacing-looking metal and wood. The difference was, a whitish, sloppy material oozed off every surface and out of every corner of this room.

"This is dough," Aryeh exclaimed, noting well the expression on Danny's face. "The monster's food you saw in the mill, that's the grain that becomes the flour that gets turned into dough. And you know what?"

Danny's bulging eyes met the baker's.

"The monster helped us to make..."

He slowly opened the oven and pulled out six steaming loaves of bread.

"It's bread," Danny whispered, spellbound.

Aryeh smiled, delighted. "Danny you have just learned how bread is made." He lowered a hand to Danny's head and gently fluffed his hair. "And, boy, oh, boy, did you learn the hard way, son."

Danny emerged from the back room with a twinkle in his eye that had all but disappeared in the last few months. At that moment, his mother knew she had her son back.

As for Aryeh, well, his mind was back on the fast track, speeding ahead at full throttle. This time his thoughts were far from Danny and his newfound knowledge. He had someone else on his mind, for he had just picked up the most powerful life lesson that had ever come his way.

14

The moonlight gave the waves a silvery sheen as they rose to splendorous crests. They hovered there for as long as they could before crashing with a strangely comforting roar that only the ocean could provide. The cool breeze that night on Clayton Beach was invigorating. It inspired Ezra to do something — he didn't know what. Staring at this vast body of water as it lapped the shores under the black, empty sky, his head filled with thoughts of the universe, of the cosmos, of Hashem orchestrating the rhythmic rush of the waves.

The absence of anything remotely brick and mortar was a relief. There were no distractions or barriers here, only the raw elements of creation as they had first appeared. It was like he could sweep human history aside for these few moments to view what lay behind it. His thoughts were free to pursue his pain without preconception or qualification. He could open it up, feel it engulf him, and let it transport him to its depths without worrying that his alarm clock would go off soon so he'd better hurry up and finish thinking about it.

The *shivah* had been the beginning of the grief and healing process, but during that week he had also been wrapped up in the grief of so many others. On the fourth day Ima had collapsed and had to be taken to hospital for an overnight stay. There were the practicalities of what to do with the baby. Thankfully Benny and his wife had stepped in, and the baby was under their care so that Ima and Abba could rest and he could get away for a short break.

It was strange to be alone in a hotel room. Whenever he had left town, it had always been with his wife, every trivial detail a shared moment: evaluating the best route, deciding on their next rest stop, the passenger handing the driver a potato chip, checking in at reception while the other hauled in the luggage, sitting on the rocks together as he did now, tossing around sand pebbles and intellectual tidbits.

The loneliness was like another dimension, with its own time zone, language, and climate. He had never been there before. It was foreign and disorienting. Although he had once been single, being married and then being single again was different. Before he was married, he was a whole entity, as whole as a single person could be, knowing he was destined to join with his soulmate. Now he was half a body, the other half chopped off of him, never to return.

The place on the rock where Devorah would have sat left an ache, much as a missing limb made known its invisible presence. It was still an automatic response to assume she was still there with him. Several times a day he would have to remind himself she was gone. Each time he did this, he was like his own Dr. Alexander, disclosing to himself the horrifying diagnosis that tore everything apart. His heart would flood with an all-encompassing pain until he would overload and had to push it all back down again. Again and again it would try to erupt, leaving him feeling like a drunkard who could not deal with his intermittent sober moments.

※ ※ ※

Considering that his mind was in such a state of flux, he had no idea how he ended up agreeing to a game of chess with the hotel manager the next morning. But the hotel was almost empty, and the manager looked lonely, so in spite of his inability to concentrate for any length of time, Ezra acquiesced.

The manager was an older man with wild puffs of white hair that looked like cumulus clouds glued to his head. He wore a conservative suit in an effort to tame his wild appearance, but it did not quite work.

They played using the giant chess pieces on the pool deck. The pieces were chipped and cracked, but they served their purpose. If the manager looked like the typical genius, it was because he was one. He trounced Ezra in a few moves, leaving Ezra's baffled mind to retrace the moves, still disbelieving that it had actually happened.

The man, George, was very serious, his heavy expression hardly changing. His skin was weathered, either from the sun or from his life. Ezra would have liked to know which.

They played again, Ezra trying this time to anticipate what brilliant ambush lay behind a seemingly innocuous move. All of George's movements were slow and deliberate, though his mind ticked faster than a silicone chip. Ezra searched the manager's face for some clue as to his next move, but the other man's muscles were steel clamps, his frown as firm as a statue's. It seemed he had trained himself that way, or something in his life had trained him that way.

It was only when George advanced his queen right to where Ezra was standing that Ezra noticed the infamous blue numbers hailing from one of the darkest corners of humankind branded into the skin of the man's arm. Ezra balked at this unnerving site. The ink still smoldered with the horror of the inscribers. It explained a lot about George, as much as Ezra could possibly understand. This was without a doubt a torment in a class of its own.

He rested an elbow on a pawn, staring at George, who stood there waiting for his opponent's next move with a mastered patience.

When asked, George made no attempt to hide anything, spewing it out mechanically like a news broadcaster. He had been the only one in his family to survive. He had witnessed the execution of his four-year-old son. After the war he remarried, but that didn't work out. And now, here he was, bearing the distinction of hotel manager on the edge of nowhere.

Ezra noticed something remarkable. All this suffering that had bombarded George had not broken him. On the contrary, it seemed to fortify him. His skin was so thick it was like a bulletproof shield. Nothing could move him.

It brought a sick feeling to Ezra's stomach. He had been instantly downsized to a whimpering toddler in the shadow of this man. How could anything compare to what George had been through? How could he sit there, forlorn, strumming his melancholy heartstrings, when a whole realm of true suffering stood right there in front of him, squeezed into the form of this tenacious old man with the puffy white hair?

They continued with the game, but Ezra could not focus. He was almost relieved to see George calmly smash him again with a quick shuffle of bishops and rooks. Ezra thanked him politely and returned to the very rocks he had scorned moments before. He stared out again into the water, trying as always to piece everything together logically, in this case to make sense of his suffering in relation to George's.

Of course he had a right to grieve, but did he have a right to feel sorry for himself? He was, like most everyone else in his generation, a pampered product of a cozy, feel-good upbringing, replete with central heating and customer-service desks. This was precisely the root of the problem — growing up with a puffed-up perspective of human needs and rights, so that one could feel totally justified in pouring out one's wrath on the waitress who was a little tardy in bringing one's espresso. Ironically, it was George, who knew the meaning of real suffering, who merely continued with his life without any self-pitying fanfare.

Ezra sat there for a long time. He was satisfied with the truth of this new realization, but it was not helping him. What could he do? He could not change the way he was brought up. Sometimes he envied people who did not think so much.

Aryeh popped into his mind, together with the cookies, the seltzer, and the dining-room table. Somehow Aryeh was able to sprinkle specks of clarity over his jumbled thoughts. Even so, Ezra had to admit, all that Aryeh had taught him, all those incisive explanations and clear distinctions, had not really penetrated. They had made perfect sense. They had resounded with unprecedented clarity, untangling a ball of countless contradictions and laying it all out systematically for him to view.

When he had been caught up in the last frenzied attempts to save Devorah's life, the ideas had meant something. They had rolled him along toward the possibility of triumph, of miraculously snatching victory from an invincible opponent. But now, after the moment of defeat, it had all soured and dissolved, depositing him back where he was in a dust cloud. That lone tenuous highway between the head and the heart was really hard to travel. He had not truly succeeded in making it all real.

☙ ☙ ☙

Twenty-three messages. Ezra pressed the button of his answering machine, wiping his brow of the cold rain that had drenched him in the few moments that he had run from the car to the front door. The trip back had been pleasant, until he had come within range of Grandridge's brewing pot of weather surprises.

There were a number of things he had to take care of right away. He had to pick up Sarah Malka, pay bills that had been waiting for him to return, get to the office at some point. The house was a mess. He scrambled to pick things up here and there while he listened to the messages. Five of the messages were from Aryeh. Obviously something was up. He picked up the phone to call his friend while trying to scrape a frying pan clean of its crusty contents.

"I need you to come over to the bakery immediately," Aryeh burst out as soon as he heard Ezra's voice.

"What's wrong?" Ezra asked.

"Nothing's wrong. Just come. There's someone...well, I'll explain it when you get here."

※ ※ ※

Aryeh was busy with a customer, although it was evident that he was anxious to close the transaction over the chocolate croissant so he could turn his attention to Ezra. There was no one else in the store except for a young boy who sat on a stool by the counter, kicking his legs into the air.

Eventually the customer left, after having paid the amount with half a jar full of pennies she had been itching to get rid of.

"Ezra." Aryeh pounced on him, dragging him by the arm in the direction of the boy. "There's someone I'd like you to meet."

Ezra and the boy stared at each other.

"Ezra, this is Danny."

"Hi, Danny."

Danny smiled shyly.

Aryeh stood back, his eyes darting between the two of them. He rubbed his hands together with glee, ignoring Ezra's raised eyebrow.

"Er...Aryeh?" Ezra gave him a puzzled look.

"You don't know what this means," Aryeh declared with a peculiar smile and a twitch of his moustache. "You have no idea what gem Hashem has sent my way."

Aryeh bent suddenly to face Danny. "Danny, remember what I said. You must tell this man everything. Are you ready?"

Danny nodded, far less keyed up than his mentor.

He started with the field, the beautiful field. He described in his own words how it had riveted him from the start. He proceeded to detail the systematic destruction of his playing field, beginning with the ruthless chopping up and tearing of the soil by the monster, on to the heartless severing of the grass by a larger monster, then to the ominous crushing of the grass by the metal machines in the monster's house, to the pillars of fire that poured from the concrete chimneys.

Danny's face still paled at the mention of the monster, not all of his fear having evaporated.

"And then...," Aryeh coached him. They had obviously practiced this before.

Danny continued, uttering each word deliberately.

He spoke of that moment in front of the oven when the bread was removed, of that happy moment of understanding. He knew now about plowing, harvesting, grinding, and baking. He knew now that the monsters were a tractor and a combine harvester. He knew now that all of that had to be done to make bread, to make something good.

Aryeh turned proudly to Ezra, his face beaming brightly.

Ezra stood quietly, looking at both of them for a very long time. He tried to smile in appreciation of this little performance, but instead found himself brushing tears from his eyes. He bowed his head, still not saying a single word.

The light radiating from Aryeh's cheeks dimmed somewhat. "Ezra, I'm sorry if I was too…"

He was interrupted by a great bear hug, and both of them wept, leaving Danny to sit there and try to figure out what on earth had just happened.

15

The vote was unanimous to stop for a cookie break. There were no customers in the store anyway, and Danny had begun to beg that the motion be pushed forward. They all sat by the counter munching silently, Ezra and Aryeh in deep thought, Danny in ardent study of the cookie shelf.

"When does Danny go home?" Ezra inquired finally.

"Well, his mother comes to pick him up in an hour, but..." Aryeh hesitated.

"What?"

Aryeh shifted in his chair. "If you really want to know, he doesn't actually...uh...exist."

"Excuse me?"

"He doesn't exist. He is a creation by the author to help you understand."

Ezra stopped munching. Both Aryeh and Danny looked at him, embarrassed.

Ezra picked up another cookie and stared at it intently. His mind was not on the cookie at all. Then suddenly his own cheeks reddened, and a smile broke across his face.

"Well, since we're being open about this, you should know

that I don't exist either. I'm also a creation by the author to help the reader understand."

"Oh!" Aryeh exclaimed. "Well, then, we are all on the same page, aren't we?"

"Quite literally."

They all had a good laugh.

"I wonder what the reader is thinking," Aryeh mused, eyes intent on his coconut cookie.

"Hopefully taking it to heart, or all this would have been for nothing."

"I know. But don't you think it's an invasion of privacy? I mean, this was supposed to be the story of someone else's tragedies and suffering, not theirs."

Ezra sighed. "You know something? Invasion of privacy or not, I think this is the best way to talk to them. Their rabbis, counselors, and friends always urge them to accept that everything is for the good. But the information remains just that – information. It doesn't penetrate. It doesn't get incorporated. It doesn't become part of who they are. I think it all boils down to making it real. Maybe this time they will consider it."

Danny finished his third cookie, brushing the crumbs off his sweater. He had an idea of what it was all about. He had an idea of what he had been created for. He began to sing. "*Ein od milvado...ein od milvado...*"

At first he sang it softly and slowly. It gained momentum when Aryeh joined in. After Ezra downed his cookie, he joined in, too, until the store and your mind reverberated with this sublime declaration of trust, that all was One, that all was good.

About the Author

Rabbi Yitzchak Goldman was born and raised in Johannesburg, South Africa, where he completed a business degree and began an investigation of his Jewish roots. What he discovered shaped his life's goals, and he attended yeshivos in Israel for several years, culminating in his rabbinical ordination and the completion of the Ohr Lagolah Outreach Training Program. With a vision of imparting to others the Torah he had learned, he joined the Seattle Kollel as a teacher and speaker, traversing the Northwest armed with Torah answers to complex issues.

In this book, he has attempted to tackle one of them, a subject that has repeatedly raised its head among a broad array of questioning minds and disillusioned hearts. He is married, and he and his wife, Sara, have three little girls.